THE STATE OF GRACE

Rachael Lucas

Feiwel and Friends

NEW YORK

A Feiwel and Friends Book

An imprint of Macmillan Publishing Group, LLC

175 Fifth Avenue, New York, NY 10010

Our books may be purchased in bulk for promotional, educational, or business use. Please contact your local bookseller or the Macmillan Corporate and Premium Sales Department at (800) 221-7945 ext. 5442 or by e-mail at MacmillanSpecialMarkets@macmillan.com.

Library of Congress Cataloging-in-Publication Data is available.

ISBN 978-1-250-12998-7 (hardcover) / ISBN 978-1-250-12999-4 (ebook)

Book design by Rebecca Syracuse

Feiwel and Friends logo designed by Filomena Tuosto

First American edition, 2018

Originally published in the United Kingdom by Pan Macmillan

1 3 5 7 9 10 8 6 4 2

fiercereads.com

To Verity.
This one was only ever for you.

CHAPTER ONE

Being a human is a complicated game—like seeing a ghost in the mirror and trying to echo everything they do. Or like walking in step, but with someone trying to trip you up—and you're juggling at the same time, with people pelting more and more balls at you. Then, just when you get the hang of it, someone starts flashing a flashlight in your eyes and then yelling in your ear.

I'll be midconversation and listening and responding in all the right places, then someone will say something on the other side of the room—a snatch of something that my brain will pick up. I'll lose the thread for a second, and when I tune back in I've lost my way. And then the other person might—for a split second—look at me oddly or scratch their nose and I'll start thinking, *No, Grace, you've lost it*, and by then I've fallen even further behind, and I remember that my face has probably stopped making the appropriate shapes (interested, listening, concerned, thoughtful—I have a full repertoire, as long as I don't get distracted), and then I panic.

And that's where it starts. We're in geography and Mrs. Dawes is talking about tectonic plates and Sarah's sitting next to me and she won't stop breathing and the clock on the wall is ticking slightly out of time with the clock that she's got on her desk and I'm trying to focus on what she's saying but it feels like the walls are collapsing in on me.

And I'm sitting there thinking—I could just walk out. Like people do in films or on television. You see it all the time. They just get up and they walk out the door and there's a slam and they just keep on walking and the rest of the pupils all look at one another in surprise and there are raised eyebrows and the teacher pushes back her chair with a screech of metal on tiled floor and a sigh of resignation and . . .

ooo

"*Obviously* we're doing everything we can for Grace. But we have the interests of the other pupils to think of and—well—behavior like this could set an unfortunate precedent."

I'm not supposed to be able to hear Mrs. Miller through the door of her office, but she's got a voice like a strangled crow, even with discretion mode activated.

The rough material covering the chair in the school foyer prickles at the backs of my knees. I run my hand across the wooden arm, tracing the shape of the heart etched into the varnish by another waiting student, sometime in the past. I've watched it fade over the years from a bright scar in the wood to a faded memory of a moment. I run my finger around and around it as I listen.

"Yes, of *course*. I appreciate your position, obviously." Mum is echoing her words carefully, using the reflective listening skills she's been working on, and that's her *oh yes, I completely understand* tone, the one she saves for teachers, counselors, support-group workers, doctors, educational psychologists . . .

"I'll have a word with Grace." I hear her pausing for a moment. "The thing is, her father is away."

There's a pause and a clattering of fingernails on laptop keyboard.

"If you *could* keep us up to date with information like this, it really would help."

I can feel the atmosphere crackle. I can imagine Mum in that second. Hands balling into fists under the table, back straightening defensively, chin rising.

"Well, I did *try* to call, Mrs. Miller." Her words sound spiky now. "But it's virtually impossible to get past the school secretary. I'm *more* than aware that change unsettles my daughter."

When Mum gets angry, she gets more clipped and posh. There's another pause before she carries on. I can imagine them glaring at each other across the desk.

"He's gone for a—well, he's . . ."

There's another beat of silence before she finishes. "He's on another contract shoot."

(Dad's not a hired killer, incidentally. He's a wildlife cameraman.) More silence.

"We've been very busy with end-of-term reports, and we have had *quite* a bit of contact already this half term regarding Grace and we're only seven weeks into the year." Defensive reply.

I know they've had meetings without me there, as well as the awkward ones where I'm dragged out of class and forced to sit in Mrs. Miller's office staring at the wall and trying to nod in all the right places. And then there's *this* kind, where I'm waiting outside, the problem they need to solve.

I curl my knees up toward my chest. It makes me feel sick when the adults start snarling at one another. I take a breath in, but it shudders through me. I can hear my heart thumping in my ears. The smell of the chair fabric is causing a headachy throb behind my eyes.

"I think it'd be best if you take her home this afternoon, have a chat. We've got the exams coming up next term, and you need to stress to her how important it is that she's focused in class. There's only another week left until the holidays."

There's a silence before she adds an afterthought—and she sounds half surprised as she says it.

"Grace is a very bright girl, you know."

I slouch down at the click of the door handle opening, making sure I look as if I'm staring absently into space, and definitely *not* eavesdropping on the whole conversation with my super-bat-hearing powers.

"Mrs. Miller and I have had a little chat."

I look at them as if I'd forgotten they existed. They fall for it and explain that under the circumstances, Grace, it's best if we just remember that we don't just walk out of the classroom, Grace, even if we are feeling a little overwhelmed. And don't forget, Grace, you can always tell the teacher if you need some time out.

It's not that easy. It's like there's a wall that stops me from saying the words, even if I need to. And that's before the whole everyone-else-looking-at-me thing, because we all know school is basically just a socially acceptable version of the Lord of the Bloody Flies. But there's something that makes saying the words *I am a bit stressed—can I please go outside to the carefully constructed quiet room?* just a tiny bit completely impossible.

Oh, and then there's the fact that the quiet room is (a) next to the cafeteria, so it smells of hot metal and thin, pointy headaches and (b) is opposite the gym hall so the *thud thud thud* of basketballs makes me want to scream. But I suppose they tried. It's a shame they didn't actually consult anyone who'd want to use it, and that's why it ends up being a glorified store cupboard with a wall stacked with props from the end-of-term performance and a stack of leftover copies of *Of Mice and Men* beside the ergonomic beanbag (hissing noise, weird smell) and a token lava lamp and some inspirational posters. And a dying plant.

Anyway. None of that matters because we're in the car now and it's one more week until half term and that means (a) I can be at the stables all week and (b) oh my God, the party. A tiny little bubble of fizzy excitement flirrups through my stomach. And yes, I know "flir-rup" isn't a word, but it is in my head. In fact, that's one of the things my best friend, Anna, likes best about me. My words always make her laugh. I like her because she's nice and she makes me laugh and she's kind and funny and she doesn't mind that I'm a bit—

"Grace, if you don't like geography, it's not too late to drop it as a subject, concentrate on the ones you like. We're only seven weeks into tenth grade."

Mum, who's been driving in silence, turns to look at me as she pauses at the junction. I'm tapping thumb against fingers, one after another, in time to the clicking noise of the blinker.

"Grace?"

I close my eyes so I can concentrate. I hear her sigh in irritation.

"Grace, you're just being bloody *rude*, and that's not okay. I've told you before if someone asks you a question you have to answer them."

We turn onto our road and the ticking stops. I open my eyes again, staring ahead. I'm counting the road signs down. NO LEFT TURNS. ONE-WAY STREET. 20. It reminds me of being four and coming home from nursery school.

"GRACE, I am sick to death of this."

After a few moments, I find my voice.

"I don't dislike geography."

We're pulling into the driveway now and I can tell she's seriously pissed off. She gets out of the car, hefting her brown bag onto her shoulder with a huff of air and slamming the door. She's marching up to the porch, not waiting for me. I climb out, deliberately slowly. The second I close the car door, she blips the car locked without looking back, and heads into the hall, leaving the front door open for me.

Withnail is there, snaking around my ankles, tail a hopeful question mark. I scoop her up and carry her through to the kitchen, where I place her on the table while I tip out a sachet of disgusting dead-animal food for her. She chirrups with delight and hops down precisely, meeting the bowl on the cold tiles of the kitchen floor.

"Mum says you're in trouble?"

There's a *clonk* as my little sister throws her bag down on the table. Her school finished early today, and she's not going to be impressed that her Netflix time has been eaten into by my returning unannounced.

Mum reappears. "Leah, I said nothing of the sort." She shoots Leah an eyebrows-down, *shut up* sort of look.

She's already tied her hair back in a ponytail, swapped her contact lenses for glasses, and replaced her shirt and posh coat with a sweatshirt.

"I don't know why you get dressed up to see Mrs. Miller. It's not like *she* makes an effort."

Mum fills the kettle and flicks it on before turning to face me. I catch a waft of Bach Rescue Remedy on her breath—if you ask me, it's just a socially acceptable way of drinking in the middle of the afternoon. The amount she goes through, she'd be better off making her own remedies by shoving a bunch of flowers in a bottle of brandy.

"I don't have to explain what I'm wearing to you, Grace. For your information," she continues, and I look at her, wondering if she realizes that's exactly what she's doing, "I happened to feel like making an effort to wear something nice because I don't have to spend every day in a shirt and a pair of leggings. I've done that for long enough. And because it's important the school recognizes I'm taking the—situation—seriously."

Leah looks up from the overflowing bowl of Coco Pops she's just poured herself. She raises her eyebrows and looks at me sideways. "You're a situation now?"

I shrug. "Apparently."

She shovels in a spoonful of cereal and crunches it noisily, which makes me feel a bit sick.

Basically, if Leah's not doing some kind of sporting thing, she's eating. She's like a one-person training montage, and I guess it uses up a lot of energy. Right now she's in her PE clothes. I can see the tangle of her blazer and school uniform balled up in her bag. (I predict that Mum will complain about that within the next half hour, once she's finished with me.)

"What've you done?" She looks at me, and then I catch her glancing at Mum. For a split second I feel like I'm on the outside of some unspoken conversation—but then I often feel like that. I think it's probably how it feels when you're really fluent in a language but you're with native speakers. I speak human as a second language, and there's always a subtext that I miss.

Mum shakes her head slightly.

"Leah, leave it."

She leans back against the kitchen counter, and looks directly at me in a way that makes me feel distinctly uncomfortable. I stare at the floor, but I can feel her eyes burning into me. It doesn't matter how many books she reads—and, believe me, she's read them *all*—she just. Doesn't. Get. It. It's physically painful to have someone staring at me like that. Her eyes burn into me and I can feel my skin prickling. Trying to escape, I step backward toward the door.

"Grace got a bit upset today. That's all. Anyway," Mum says, in the cheerful voice that always indicates that she's gathered herself and decided not to make a fuss about whatever I've done wrong, "how about dinner in front of the TV, and hot chocolate and pj's?"

"Can we have those cookies?" Leah knows we've got Mum over a barrel this week. "The chocolate ones you hid in the garage?"

"How did you know about them?"

I raise my eyes in time to see Leah pull a face. "We know everything, Mother. It's our job."

The truth is Mum went on a major comfort-food shopping trip the night that Dad left for Greenland. She came home loaded with chocolate-caramel-covered everything, about fifty-seven tubs of Häagen-Dazs, and a crate of red wine, which she locked in the garage, where the freezer and all the food worth eating lives. She keeps the key on her at all times. She's been even stressier than usual for some reason since Dad went this time, and she keeps snapping.

Anyway, I'm happy to watch whatever she wants on television (even if I'll be reading my book at the same time) if it means chocolate.

ooo

Where were you? Waited at the flagpole until ten past.

My phone's on silent because we're supposed to be having Quality Family Time, which means no contact with the outside world, but I catch it glowing sideways through the cushion where I've stuffed it out of sight. It's Anna. Oh God. When Mum took me home, I completely forgot to tell her I wasn't going to be there. My stomach gives a glurp of anxiety and I hold my breath as I reply.

Got picked up. REALLY sorry.

I don't want to go into the whole walking-out-of-class thing, and she's not in my geography class. I don't want to think about it at all, actually, because when I do I get that weird swooping horrible feeling in my stomach and my skin goes all fizzy just thinking about it. And I'm gnawing on my thumbnail waiting for her to reply. I'm worried that she might just think *sod it*, because, honestly, she could. Anytime. I have no idea why she's friends with me, because Anna's *lovely*. She's sort of accepted by the populars and the jocks and the geeks *and* the funny in-betweeny ones—and even with all that she still chooses to be my best friend, even though I must bring her down about fifty nerd points in the universal school scale of social acceptability.

No stress. But . . . party crisis. WTF are we going to wear?

And with one sentence the prickly skin feeling is gone and my heart settles down with a little thump, like a stone landing at the bottom of a pond.

Mum's fallen asleep on the sofa, where Leah's lying beside her with her thumb in her mouth (even though she's thirteen, don't ask) staring at an old episode of *Friends* like she's about to take an exam in it. I get up, unplugging my charger, and slip out of the room as Anna messages again.

You doing anything tomorrow? Come around to mine and we can try some stuff on. I'll do your hair?

CHAPTER TWO

love Anna's bedroom, because it's not mine, so the mess doesn't feel so messy. And she's much better at lining up her posters and she doesn't have a dressing table that looks like an explosion in a nail-polish factory. And she didn't carve the names of JLS on her mirror when she was nine, so she doesn't have to live with the reminder every time she puts on eyeliner that she used to be in love with a crap boy band. Saying that, she does have One Direction stuck on the back of the bedroom door. I know because, when the door closes, her bathrobe swings sideways and Harry Styles peeks out from under the sleeve.

"What about leggings and denim shorts?"

I pick them up from the tangle of clothes on the bed, and wave them at her hopefully.

"Too short."

We're only invited to Charlotte Regan's party because Anna's mum works in the health center with Charlotte's mum, and they're friends. They still haven't quite grasped the idea that just 'cause we were friends in nursery school doesn't mean we're going to hang out ten years later. But anyway, whatever Charlotte's mum said (something along the lines of *You're only having a party if Anna and Grace come because they're so completely überdorky, particularly Grace, that there is NO CHANCE of anything even vaguely scandalous happening*), we're invited to the Party of the Year.

Charlotte's family lives in a farmhouse three miles out of town, and her sixteenth birthday party is taking place in the barn. It's going to be all sitting-around-on-straw-bales and like something out of a film. Or so everyone says. It's been all anyone's talked about since we got over Tom Higginson falling off his brother's motorbike and breaking both ankles.

"Grace?"

I look up, realizing Anna's been talking for at least a minute. She's wearing a pair of ripped black jeans and a skinny purple T-shirt with a kitten-fluffy black cardigan, which makes her red hair look like flames on her shoulders. (She doesn't mind "red," hates "ginger," prefers "auburn"—but she's totally living in fantasy land, because it's *orange* and it is AMAZING and I would love orange hair.) Anyway, she looks like she'd fit in perfectly with the super-cool gang and I feel a horrible pang of something in my stomach. For a second I don't say anything, because I always, always, always feel like I'm panting to keep up with her and I always have been, ever since we made friends when she helped me wash the paintbrushes at Little Acorns when we were three.

"It's perfect." I say the words brightly. Then I do a sort of half frown because I'm not sure that it didn't sound a bit sharp.

Anna gathers her orange hair in a bunch and sort of balls it in her fist, frowning, like she's not sure where it all came from. "You think?"

I nod. And Anna flashes a really sweet smile. It's a smile that says *thank you for being my friend* and *thank you for saying I look nice* and I know that I got it right. It's not that I don't want to get it right, it's just . . . God, it's hard work being a person sometimes. I floomp down sideways onto the fluffy pillows at the head of her bed and breathe in the fake plastic smell of them, which reminds me of inflatable toys and a trip to Singapore we made when I was seven.

"Grace?"

I take my head back out of Singapore.

"What about you?"

Argh. If I'm honest, I want to wear my favorite black jeans and my mum's ancient, slightly holey Pixies T-shirt she had when she was seventeen. And my gray hoodie, and my Vans with a hole in the toe. But I'm guessing that's not in the rules. I might just pack the T-shirt in my bag in case I need a comfort sniff of it at the party when it all gets a bit . . . well, people-y. Parties are a bit like that, even if they don't have Pass the Parcel and organized fun.

Anna holds out a bright red T-shirt with a My Little Pony on the front.

"It's ironic," she points out helpfully, "and I've got to face the fact that I can't wear red and must stop buying it." She thrusts it at me, waving it in my face.

"If I wear it, it's not going to look ironic. I'll just look like a complete loser with a My Little Pony obsession."

I giggle and she throws the T-shirt at my head so I can't see. I feel her landing on the bed beside me with a thump and a snort of laughter, which doesn't quite mask the splintery noise of bed slats cracking in half.

"Thing one," says my friend, removing the T-shirt from my head and throwing it so it hurtles toward the wall. It slides out of sight behind the chest of drawers, where it'll be eaten by a million lost hair bands or move in with a family of dust bunnies, "you *are* a complete loser with a My Little Pony fetish—that's why we're friends. How many do you own?"

I hide my face behind a cushion so all she can see are my eyes peeping over the top.

"And thing two: slightly more urgent. We just broke the bed."

I can already hear Anna's mum making her way upstairs, and they're not the footsteps of a happy parent.

"You can talk." I point to the row of dusty Barbie dolls that balance, their legs swinging back and forth like a line of retired Mean Girls, on top of Anna's wardrobe. "At least my ponies are in a box under the bed. I keep my weird habits private." I stick my tongue out at Anna just as the door bangs open so hard that Harry Styles bangs against the edge of the bookcase and Anna's bathrobe falls off the hook.

"Oops, sorry. Pushed it with my foot. Do you girls want some cake?" Anna's mum doesn't seem to be upset at all, weirdly. In fact, she's wielding a plate with two fat slices of gingerbread with thick white icing on top.

"Do you need to ask?" Anna shuffles carefully forward, clearly trying not to give away the fact that the mattress underneath her is now sagging in the middle.

"Darling, are you all right?" Anna's mum cocks her head to one side, looking at me for confirmation. "Grace, is she going mad? Is there something I should know about?"

I shake my head, feeling the laughter threatening to escape, lips tightly clamped together. Sometimes when I start it's so hard to stop and then Anna joins in and we just laugh and laugh until we're almost sick. We got sent out of English last week for snortling with laughter over *"Thou cream-faced loon"* in Shakespeare.

I can feel it boiling up inside me, and any second now I'm going to start. Anna's shoulders are beginning to shake.

"It's just . . ." Anna grasps the fail-safe method of shutting up all adults, at all times. *"Women's problems."*

"Ohhh," says Anna's mum with a knowing nod. "Definitely time for cake, then, darling. D'you want some medicine or something?"

"No-I'm-fine," says Anna in a rush, as the bed gives another warning creak.

"All right. Let me know if you want anything."

And she pulls the door closed as she backs out of the room, brow wrinkled in an expression of bemusement, half shaking her head at the weirdness of us, and we fall over on our sides and laugh and laugh until the bed finally gives way underneath us and Anna's legs shoot upward as her bum sinks to the floor.

ooo

It's a couple of hours later. I'm hovering in Anna's kitchen, staring out of the window and talking to her cat, Michael. Anna is upstairs with her mum, who apparently has psychic powers or something, because she returned half an hour later, this time without cake, but with a tool-box. She made us move the mattress into the hall while she fixed the broken slats in the bed frame. We were too weak with laughter to argue, and we tried to make up for it by getting her a cup of tea and offering to hold pieces of equipment, but she just rolled her eyes at us and told us to sod off.

I wonder if that's why Anna and I are friends: because we both have the sort of mothers who just get on with stuff. Because Dad's always worked away—he spends months balancing behind his lens, waiting for the perfect photograph of an antelope doing a cartwheel (or something like that)—Mum's always been the one who does all the stuff. She bosses us around and organizes everything and remembers appointments and buys stuff for cookery class on the way to school when I forget. Thing is, when Dad *is* around he's on another planet too, holed up in his study editing hours of footage and collecting coffee cups and chip bags. And Anna's dad is the same—lovely, but not exactly practical. He's an engineer, so he ought to be, really. He spends a lot of time in his office looking at very complicated pictures of stuff on his computers, which we're not allowed to touch.

And we both have cats with cool names, so there's another reason why we're friends. And then there's our mutual interest in the mysterious Gabe Kowalski. He arrived halfway through the summer term from one of the other schools in town. Someone said he's got A Reputation, but I'm not really sure what that means. He seemed per-

14

fectly nice when he picked up Anna's sneaker—it fell out of her bag last term—and he smiled and said, "There you are," reeeeeally nicely in his lovely accent.

Friendship is a weird sort of thing when you think about it.

I look at the calendar on the wall above the kitchen sink, scanning the details that Anna's mum has written in her neat, spidery black writing.

It'd be useful for their parents if Anna and *Charlotte* were friends, really. "Lunch with Adam and Gillian," it says for tomorrow. They're Charlotte's parents. Anna hasn't mentioned it. I know that's not because she's keeping it as a special secret and she's planning on running off to be best friends with Charlotte, because Anna is one of my safe places. She's one of the things that doesn't move and doesn't change. That's a good thing.

What's *not* a good thing is standing here in the kitchen feeling faintly worried that I'm going to be in trouble because Anna broke the bed. Even though Anna's mum's mouth said it was fine, her face said, *Oh, for God's sake, I've got better things to do than fix this bloody bed.*

I recognize the look. My mum gets exactly the same one on her face when we break stuff.

"All sorted." Anna's mum comes back into the kitchen, putting the toolbox down on the table with a thump, all the tools inside banging together in a metallic, teeth-on-edge crash. It makes me jump and another wave of anxiety rushes through my body, sending me cold from my toes to my head in a whoosh of panic.

"You all right, my love?" Anna's mum makes her way across the wooden floor toward me and puts her hand on my arm. I stiffen up. I don't mean to—it's just I'm reaching the point where everything's a bit too *much* everything and I'd like to magically be back home in bed with a heap of blankets. I shiver, even though the room is warm. I just need to get home. Now. But I don't say that.

I say:

"I'm fine."

I realize I'm drumming my fingers against the counter and it probably looks like I'm impatient. It's not that; I'm just tapping the rhythm of an ancient Beyoncé song for some reason that makes no sense, but I can't stop it because it's weirdly soothing. *Taptaptaptap* break *tap tap* break *taptaptap*.

"Do you need a lift home?" She gives my fingers a fleeting glance for the tiniest second and I notice it and hold them still. The rhythm shifts to my toes and now each one of them is beating their turn (but she can't see that bit).

She turns to look for Anna, who is nowhere to be seen—probably putting the bed back together. I feel super awkward all of a sudden, like my arms and legs are too big for my body and they're going to keep growing like the magic porridge pot until they take over the whole kitchen.

"Oh no, my mum's just coming," I reply after a moment, realizing that I'd forgotten to say the words out loud. "She's on her way back from town, said she'd pick me up on the way past."

The doorbell rings and Anna comes hurtling down the stairs, shouting that she'll get it.

"Gracie Moo, your mum is here." She does a cartwheel in the hall, which makes her mum pull the sort of face I imagine mother dragons pull when their children are naughty. Her nostrils go all snorty.

"Anna, will you *keep* that behavior outside. For goodness' sake, you're fifteen, not five."

Anna flashes a grin at her mum then catches my eye as she swings onto the kitchen table, picking up an apple from the fruit bowl.

"Make your mind up, Mother." She spoke through a mouthful of apple. "Yesterday you were all full of woe that I'm growing up too fast. Now you're telling me off for being youthfully exuberant."

"You've broken a bed and now you're doing acrobatics in the hall," she said pointedly. "I think under the circumstances I'm allowed to be a bit annoyed."

Her mum looks at mine and shakes her head.

"These two." She half moves toward the kettle. "Got time for a cuppa before you go?"

Mum wavers for a second.

"Go on, then." She pulls her phone out of the back pocket of her jeans. "I'll text Leah, tell her we'll be half an hour. Thanks, Lisa."

She sits down at the big wooden table while Lisa clatters around with coffee cups.

"Have you girls been behaving?"

Mum says this to me, but looks at Anna's mum with that look mothers reserve for each other. I feel about seven.

"They've been perfect angels." I feel a wave of love for Anna's mum and her kind voice and her not minding that we bounced the bed in half after all. My mum snorts with laughter.

Anna, who has been teasing Michael the cat with a feather, looks up at me, motioning toward the door with her head. We can escape.

"So how long's he gone for this time?" Lisa slides a coffee across the table toward my mum.

As we leave, I hear my mum telling Lisa it'll be almost Christmas before my dad is back. She sounds distinctly unimpressed.

∘∘∘

"Come on, you," says Mum, an hour later.

"You've been ages." I hoist myself out of the gigantic squashy sofa, plonking Michael onto Anna's lap.

"And now it's time to go. Leah's been texting, asking where we are."

"I'll message you," says Anna, waving Michael's paw at me in farewell.

∘∘∘

And then we're home. And I've done enough everything for today. I've been enough. I have literally no Graceness left to offer anyone or anything. I'm wrapped up in my fleece blanket like a burrito and it's safe and warm and I'm watching *Walking with Dinosaurs* on Netflix for the fifty billionth time. I just want to sit here all evening, because then my brain might just stop whirring around. It's like a million shooting stars flying out in different directions and I can't make them stop and then I can't sleep. The dinosaurs help. The beanie hat I've got on helps too. It sort of stops the thoughts from shooting around.

ooo

I can't sleep. It's after midnight, and I've read the whole internet and I've had a shower and watched so many trashy American TV shows that my brain is beginning to melt, and I'm starving.

As I'm creeping down the stairs, trying not to wake anyone up, I realize there's a noise coming from the sitting room. I open the door to find Mum. She's sitting on the couch in her pajamas, and Nirvana is on old-people MTV, and there's a bottle of red wine three-quarters drunk by her side. She looks up, head cocked to hold her cell phone in place under her ear, and beams at me fuzzily.

"Hello, darling. I'm just rediscovering my lost youth."

She giggles as presumably someone on the end of the phone says something. "Shh," she says to them, waving a hand pointlessly. "You okay?" She looks at me quizzically.

"Fine." Withnail is curled up on a fluffy tartan blanket at Mum's feet and the fire is still glowing from earlier. I like it when the fire's lit—it makes the house feel alive somehow, like it's got a personality. "Just getting food."

She nods, and turns back to the television and her phone as I withdraw.

I had no idea she could get Dad on the phone from Greenland, but I can't think who else she'd be talking to at this time of night. The floor's freezing, so I sit on the kitchen counter as I wait for the toast, shoving over a heap of Mum's paperwork as I do so. She doesn't work, but the voluntary stuff she does with the local autism support group takes over her entire life. Maybe she was talking to one of her cronies from there.

The toaster pops, and I stop thinking about anything else apart from melty butter deliciousness.

I'll clean the mess up in the morning.

CHAPTER THREE

Sometimes I wonder what it'd be like to be one of those people who sleep until midday on the weekend. At six in the morning our kitchen is silent, apart from the pop and click of the kettle switching off and the fizz of instant coffee as I fill the travel mug.

Screwing the lid on tightly, I shove it in my backpack and hitch it over one shoulder. I'm sure they'll know where I am—I'm a creature of habit, after all—but I'm getting better at this stuff, so I leave a note, scrawled on the back of an envelope, lying next to the toaster on a heap of last night's crumbs, which I've forgotten to clean up, but never mind.

I pull the door behind me and my bike clatters down the front steps as if eager to get away. It's a funny sort of half-light at this time of the morning, and the town feels like it doesn't quite belong to anyone—night has handed it over, but daytime isn't quite here yet and there's only me, and the almost-silent whirring of the milk truck that's waiting outside the houses opposite.

And then I'm in the yard and everything is forgotten. The stables are a sanctuary. The routine—the way every day is the same, no matter what's going on in the outside world—is part of why I love it here. I throw my backpack down in the tack room and pick up the kettle, shaking it from side to side. It's still warm—Polly must be here already. I'll have a coffee when I get back from the field.

○○○

Mabel's there, as if she read my mind. I reach across the fence, holding my hand out, palm flat, feeling the velvet whiskeryness of her muzzle as she softly sniffs me hello. I don't bother putting on a lead rein or a halter when there's nobody around to tell me off—she doesn't need it. I open the gate and she slips through gracefully, one ear flicking backward as she senses the other members of the herd looking up.

Together, side by side, we walk up to the yard, her hooves clipping precisely as we step from the earth of the track onto the concrete. I open the door to her stable and she steps inside.

When I'm with Mabel, everything melts away. I forget about the coffee. I brush her silver-gray mane until each strand shines like spun silk. When she's groomed, I shove her grooming kit back into the cupboard under the feeding trough and pull out her saddle and bridle, tacking her up quickly. I want to be out while it's still early, before the rest of the world comes alive, and we make it, a plaintive whinny from Mabel's best friend, Harry, sounding out across the field as we disappear from sight.

There's nothing in the pink silence of the morning but a gentle clinking as Mabel chews on her snaffle bit. We turn down onto the bridle path, startling a hare, which stops, front paws in midair, before shooting off into the hedgerow. The leaves are sparkling with dew, my breath and Mabel's puffing in air as the thin sun breaks through the clouds.

Spring and autumn are my favorite times to be outside. And winter, when it's cold and the sitting room is full of the sparkly darkness of fairy lights and candles on the fireplace. But not summer. Summer's too obvious, too yellow, too shiny and easy to please. It doesn't have to try too hard, and everyone just loves it anyway.

We're as one, Mabel and me. Her ears are pricked forward, questing, the dark gray tips curving in toward each other, her mane flying gracefully, neck curved in an arc. The repetitive rhythm of the trot has me counting one-two-one-two like Penny, my riding instructor, used to when I was seven and having lessons. I realize I'm muttering it under my breath as we reach the top of the little hill.

The trees here have been sawn away by the forestry workers, exposing circles of startled pale wood, the ground still blanketed with fallen needles. I pull Mabel to a stop and slide off, hooking her reins around my hand. I've got a packet of mints and I'm training her to take one from my mouth. I balance the sweet between my lips and she reaches out gently, her mushroom-soft top lip catching it and knocking it to the ground. She hoovers it up instantly. We're working on it.

Anna, who appreciates Mabel—but from a distance—thinks it's disgusting that I'd let a horse snuffle all over my face.

But I love Mabel with the heat of a million suns. She's standing silhouetted in the golden light of early morning, her profile as beautiful as her desert ancestors, nostrils flaring in a sigh of contentment. I reach up, placing a hand against the flatness of her cheekbone, sending a silent message.

Thank you. Thank you for letting me be your person. Thank you a million times for the day they said, *We've decided you can have a horse of your own.* I can't say the words out loud, but I feel them pulsing through me and into the warmth of her skin.

And then there's a crash, which sends Mabel wheeling and snorting to the end of the reins, my arm jerking as she pulls away from me, the tips of her ears almost meeting in the middle, her nostrils flaring, neck rigid with shock.

"Shit."

There's a voice behind me.

There's a metallic sound and a groan. As I turn, I see a mountain bike emerging from the ditch, followed by a soaking-wet, mud-splattered arm, followed by—

"Jesus. What are you doing up here at this time of the morning?"

The voice comes first before a shape clambers over the bank, its face completely covered in mud, water dripping from the visor of his—it's a he, I realize—helmet. He hauls himself out over the edge of the bank and looks at me through his mud mask, wiping his face with the hem of his sweatshirt. I'm so hopeless at recognizing people out of context that it takes me a second before I recognize the dark brown eyes staring out from the mud-covered face.

"It's a bridle path. And this"—I indicate the highly unimpressed Mabel, still stock-still, who gives a well-timed huff of disapproval—"is my horse. Wearer of a bridle. Hence the path."

Shut up, Grace, for God's sake.

Gabe Kowalski looks down at the slightly mangled bike, which is lying beside him on the grass.

"Right," he says, and he's laughing. "Did you have sarcasm flakes for breakfast?"

I thought I was simply stating the obvious. Not sure what to say, I carry on looking at him as he clambers to his feet, frowning down at the bike wheel.

"I'm not being sarcastic," I manage eventually. "It's just—what on earth are *you* doing riding a mountain bike into a ditch?"

"It wasn't exactly in the plan. I was coming down the hill and the ditch just sort of—appeared. And then we—me and the bike—were in it."

He gives a sheepish smile. One front tooth crosses over the other, I notice.

"D'you need a hand?" I step forward, but Mabel has other ideas. She's rooted to the spot and she's not moving one inch. She's got no concept of sisterhood, this horse.

"Looks like your transport isn't behaving any better than mine." He hauls the bike upright. "It'll be fine, just need to get it home and fix the forks."

"If you take the path down there"—I wave my arm in the direction of the stables—"there's a shortcut back to Lane End."

"Past the stables?" He's holding on to the bike now, readying himself to leave.

"Yes." I don't know why I don't say, *Oh, that's where I keep Mabel.* Or even, *That's where I'm headed—do you want to walk with me?*

I couldn't really say that (even if it wasn't a lie, because it's not where I'm headed, obviously), because Mabel is utterly convinced that the bike is some kind of evil swamp monster designed to murder her in her sleep, but even so, I can tell this is one of these moments where if I were in a film I'd say something cute, and so would he, and then he'd wipe the mud off his face and we'd walk home together chatting and . . .

"See you, then." He jerks his head upward as a sort of good-bye, and heads back down the track toward home.

"Yeah," I say, realizing as I do that Anna and I are going to replay this conversation a million times. "See you."

I watch him wheeling the bike, the damaged front wheel in the air, down the track toward the stables, until he's a tiny speck in the distance and Mabel's nudging me in the back, the metal of her bit jingling, and then I get back into the saddle and ride on, up to the moor.

The hollow thudding of her hooves on the peat turf and the occasional whoop of the birds overhead are the only things I can hear. It's not exactly helpful. My thoughts are spinning around and around inside my head, my brain going over all the amusing things I could have said. Like, *Hello, I'm Grace. We're in opposite sections, so we don't share any classes, but it's nice to meet you.* That might've been a start. Instead, just for a change, I've gone for socially awkward, as usual. A vision of me at Charlotte's party, standing in a corner, trying to look like I'm mysterious and interesting instead of a total loser with no social skills pops into my head and I feel a bit sick.

I'm looking forward to the party. Keep telling yourself that, Grace.

I am.

I loosen the reins and Mabel, reading my mind, soars forward into a canter and I lose myself in the thrumming of hoofbeats and the wind in my face.

CHAPTER FOUR

t's Monday. Again.

There's a smell in here that's making it impossible to concentrate. I'm vaguely aware that Miss Jones is saying something, but I can't pick it out among the stink. It's overwhelming.

"GRACE!"

I open my eyes. Tabassum, who has—I've just realized—been nudging me, lets out a resigned sigh. She knows what's coming next.

"What?"

Holly Carmichael, who sits opposite me, mutters, "Weirdo," under her breath. I don't look at her. I haven't looked her in the eye since she deliberately wrecked my donkey painting in third grade, just because it was loads better than hers. I'm aware that sounds ridiculous, but we all have coping mechanisms, and not looking at people is one of mine. I don't imagine she's even noticed—I'm not exactly on her radar these days. I'm just glad she's forgotten the time I peed in my pants at her fifth birthday party because I was having a meltdown and the balloons were scaring me.

"Don't you 'what' me, my girl." Miss Jones is approaching the table now, her mouth set in a straight line. She slams her palm down on the table so my books all jump in the air. Holly makes a *wooooo* sound, which makes the rest of the class laugh. I reach a hand forward to straighten the books, but Tabassum kicks me under the table.

The smell's coming from outside, I realize, as I see a man jumping down from the low roof of the PE storage sheds. They're sticking something down and the gluey smell has adhered to my nostrils and it's making me want to throw up. And I've just realized she's still talking.

". . . a whole class here, Grace, and I can't keep interrupting to deal with you if you can't keep on task and I . . ."

I reach into my pocket. I can't concentrate on a word she's saying and it's all in the textbook anyway.

"Miss . . ." Tabassum begins hesitantly.

I shoot her a look. There's no point even trying to explain when she's on a roll. I pull out the time-out card so it's tucked in my palm and hand it to Miss Jones, standing up as I do so. I don't have to stay here. I'm going to the library to read about the circulatory system in peace.

"Sit down."

"I've got a time-out card." I say this almost under my breath, turning away so that the only people who can hear me are the teacher and Tabassum. It's not a state secret, but my parents seem to think life will be easier if my autism is on a need-to-know basis. I'm not sure it works, but nobody bothered to ask me. So the teachers know, and most of my friends, but—

"I don't care what you've got, young lady." Miss Jones looks down at the card again, and back at me. She's got a sort of wart thing on her forehead, and there's a speck of mascara on her cheek. "You're not leaving my class."

I knew this would happen when Miss Young laminated this time-out card. Half the teachers are terrified in case I start climbing on the tables or setting fire to the desks. But the old-school ones—and they're not old-wrinkly-old; some of them are the youngest teachers we've got here—think it's just a cop-out, an excuse for me to disappear out of class before anyone realizes I haven't done my homework. The irony is I always do my homework, because I'm terrified of getting into trouble. But trouble just keeps getting into me.

I can feel everyone looking now, getting ready for something to gossip about over lunch. The silence is roaring in my ears and their eyes are all on me, all over me. I feel hot and cold and sick.

"If you're feeling *stressed*, Grace"—in what I assume is her attempt to tick the box and do the right thing, she has lowered her voice to a whispered hiss, her face rigid with fury—"why don't you turn the chair around to face the wall?"

"What?"

Have we gone back to the Victorian times? I can't concentrate on a thing she's saying because the smell is screaming in my head and everything I have is focusing on not throwing up on the table, and she wants me to face the *wall*?

"What?" I repeat it, scrunching up my face to indicate I literally do not get it.

"You mean 'pardon.'" The words are sharp-edged. They feel like broken glass.

"I don't mean 'pardon,' *actually*. If you'd read Nancy Mitford"—which I did last summer at Grandma's house, when I was completely obsessed with British manners and all that stuff, but I digress—"*you'd* know that saying 'pardon' is incredibly rude. So—for that matter—is 'toilet' instead of 'bathroom,' and 'serviette' instead of 'napkin,' and—"

A vein stands out on Miss Jones's forehead, and I watch her face turn puce with fury.

I don't turn my chair around. I don't throw up on the table. I sit for the remaining twenty-five minutes with my nails digging into my palms, everything shut down so I don't hear a word she says, and then when the class is over I turn around to pick up my stuff, but because I'm stressed and hungry—and, well, because I'm me—I drop my bag and the contents spill out all over the floor.

And because my life is only like the crappy bits of films, as I'm scrabbling around on the tiles shoving it all back in, I realize that there is a pair of immaculate black shoes standing in my way and I follow them up and there's Holly Carmichael, and she's holding something in her hand.

It's my time-out card.

Holly taps it thoughtfully on her palm, her head cocked slightly to one side. She looks down at it for a moment, thinking. I can feel my heart racing, and my stomach lurches as if I'm going to throw up.

She looks at me, her eyebrows raised. Her voice is dripping with scorn.

"You don't look autistic."

"And *you* don't look ignorant. And yet here we are."

She gives a snort, half turning as if to check her harpies are all still in place (which they are, flanking her on either side, like airheaded, gum-cracking henchmen).

I snatch the card from her hand and march out of the room before she has a chance to answer.

As soon as I turn the corner, I flop back against the wall of the science corridor and start to laugh.

Yes. Yes, yes, YES. I've had that bloody comeback stored away in my armory forever. Stuff you, Holly Carmichael.

CHAPTER FIVE

t's only the middle of the week—and I shouldn't complain, because we're being dismissed at lunchtime on Friday—but I am so tired. Tired-to-my-bones tired. The teachers are wound up about exams as usual, and the special-needs coordinator is stressing out about me having somewhere quiet to do my practice test. The room she wants to put me in is right next to the science lab and it stinks, but I couldn't face the conversation, so I just nodded when she suggested it. I'm so tired I've run out of words. Mum picked me up from school and she must've gotten it somehow, because I flopped into the back seat and she called Polly and asked her to look after Mabel this evening, and she didn't ask me how my day had been, or expect anything but silence. Lucky, because I don't have any words left.

"Come on." Mum fiddled around with the CDs in the side pocket of the car as we left school. "We'll take the coast road home."

It takes twice as long to drive this way, but it's nice, because the car is one of the places I feel safe, and where I can turn my brain off.

And I'm glad Mum gets it. She might make me want to scream sometimes, but she is good at recognizing when I've hit the wall and keeping me from losing it.

It makes me think about being small. When Leah was a tiny little pink blob in a car seat, Mum used to take us out in the car and drive around and around town, along the long shore road with the bleached grass of the dunes and the huge sky stretching out beside us. I remember the music playing and my blue shoes sticking out into the air and the same songs playing over and over, because it was the only thing I'd let her listen to.

She'd drive and drive, until Leah would fall asleep, and she'd sing along to Avril Lavigne, and she says I used to too, and it became *Grace's Avril music*, soundtrack to a million afternoons.

Only now it's more than a decade ago, and Mum's not singing this time—she's driving in silence. I don't mind, because the last thing I need is any more noise in my head. Leah's got netball training, so she doesn't need picking up for ages yet. She chose to go to the school on the other side of town, the one with the award-winning sports teams. If it weren't for the fact that she looks like a smaller, neater, less scribbly version of me, I'd be convinced Leah had been swapped at birth.

I let my eyes stop focusing. Outside becomes a blur, passing by the car windows.

I rest my head against the glass.

The trouble is that by this time my filtering system has broken down completely and there's a light flickering in the corner of my eye and the plastic smell of the car is giving me a headache right behind my eyes.

"Grace?" Mum's voice breaks through my thoughts. We've pulled up outside Leah's school.

ooo

Dinner's in front of the television tonight because Dad's program is on. I'm curled up in my chair, with a cushion on my knees and a bowl of pasta balanced on top. Mum's got a row of tea lights flickering along the mantelpiece, and the fire's lit—it's only October, and the weather forecaster said we're going to have an Indian summer this week, but it looks pretty, anyway. And autumn is waiting to catch us—I see it when I'm out riding Mabel. The fields have been plowed and the grass on the edges is faded and tired. A bit like me tonight.

Leah is sitting on the sofa beside Mum, who is clutching the remote control so tightly her knuckles are going white. She's upset—I think because she was half hoping Dad would call tonight before his show went out, even though he's already told her it's virtually impossible to ring to order when he's floating around on an iceberg, or whatever he's doing this week.

"Right?" Mum looks at me.

"Ready when you are." I hate missing the beginning of programs. If I do, I won't watch them at all. Same with the cinema. I like to be in my seat before the ads start, and I stay until the end of the credits, long after the lights have gone up and the usher is tidying up the sweet wrappers and strewn popcorn. It's just one of my things.

"The tortoise of the Galápagos Islands is an intriguing creature . . ." begins the voice from the screen.

I curl my hands around my bowl of pasta and sit forward in my chair, fascinated.

Dad's been disappearing on wildlife shoots for as long as I can remember. He'd be there, then he'd be gone, then he'd come home with a gigantic stuffed cheetah (toy, not actual animal, obviously) or whatever, and we'd all sit watching his programs together. But in the last couple of years he's been away a lot more, probably half the year, and, unlike this one, the shoot he's on at the moment is special, because he's going to be narrating it too, so it'll be like he's here in the room.

Leah's got her phone tucked under the cushion beside her on the sofa. I can see she's messaging with one hand while eating dinner and looking innocent with the other. She's become a complete social-media addict over the last few months, and Mum and Dad haven't noticed. Mum, meanwhile, is halfway down a glass of red and has barely touched her pasta. She's flipping a coaster between her fingers, and she looks cross—or maybe tired? I can't really tell.

I flick a piece of my pasta across the chair so it lands on the arm beside Withnail.

"Grace, if you're feeding that cat at the table again, he's going out." Mum doesn't even look across at me.

"We're not *at* the table."

I flip another twirl of pasta out and sneak it into my palm for him to have in a moment. He's started his motorbike purr of delight in anticipation. How can I deprive him of his favorite thing? (Besides chips, cheese, strawberry yogurt, and Christmas cake, but you know what I mean.)

"GRACE."

"FINE." God, she's in a mood. Meanwhile, Leah's doing whatever the hell she likes right under her nose.

"Who were you talking to earlier when Grace was in the shower?" Leah looks at Mum, mouth stuffed full of pasta. I swear our carb-wolfing qualities are in the blood, with Mum being half-Italian. "Was it Dad?"

Mum shakes her head.

"Grandma?"

"I do have *friends*, you know," Mum says, and she sounds a bit sharp.

"Who?" I look across at her, interested. The turtles are still doing their thing on the television—between you and me, they're not that interesting, and I speak as someone who's watched more nature nerd programs than anyone I know.

"For goodness' sake, you two." She sounds a bit huffy now. "If you must know, it was my friend Eve from university."

She's never mentioned an Eve before. I wonder if that's who she was talking to the other night when I went into the sitting room. But she can say she's got friends all she wants . . . the truth is that basically all Mum does is be a mum. And do her volunteer stuff at the center. And attend classes on How to Parent Your Autistic Child. And read books on the same. Meanwhile I just get on with being myself, because nobody actually gives you a guidebook on How to Be an Autistic Person. Anyway, it seems to keep her occupied.

"But you said 'see you later' to this Eve person." Leah slides me a look.

"Ooh, look, pause it—rewind it! There's Dad." I wave my arm at the television where, for a brief moment, he pops into view, and I feel a weird, gulping sense of missing him that makes my cheeks ache.

Mum sighs and hits the rewind button. We all sit forward in our chairs for a moment, peering at the screen, not speaking.

"Well, there we are," says Mum, taking a big mouthful of her wine. "That's the closest you two will get to a bedtime story from your father this evening." Her face twists a bit into an expression I don't recognize, and we all sit back with our pasta and watch the rest of the program without talking. There's a weird feeling in the air that makes me feel unsettled. When the show is finished, I get up and take the bowls through to the kitchen, Withnail following me for his share of leftover pasta.

I can hear Mum and Leah laughing at some comedy thing on the television now, but I've had enough of today. I climb the stairs and don't even bother getting into my pajamas, because I've only got to get my uniform on again in the morning and I'll brush my teeth later, and I stuff my headphones into my ears and turn the world off and Taylor Swift on.

I don't mean cool, hanging-out-with-her-squad-in-NYC, everyone-loves-her Taylor Swift. I mean Taylor Swift from when I was little and I wanted her ringlets. That's what I want to listen to. I pull the covers over my head and hit repeat on my phone so it plays over and over and over again like an aural comfort blanket until I've forgotten everything else, and I'm living somewhere in Tennessee and my mom is making pancakes with maple syrup as an after-school surprise.

CHAPTER SIX

"We need face masks."

We're in Costa having a hot chocolate and it's Friday after school and it's half term at last. And that also means it's THE PARTY at last and not that we're excited or anything but Anna's written a list of Things We Have to Do and printed it off, because Anna is the queen of stationery and notebooks and paper in general.

I do sometimes wonder whether I sneezed one day and she caught autism from me, or at least the bits everyone reads about, because unlike her I've never written a list in my life, and I'm hopeless at math, and I don't have a special superpower like drawing entire cityscapes from memory.

"Look." Anna taps the list with an impatient finger. "Face masks. Hair-conditioning treatments. Manicure stuff."

"Y'know Gabe?" I try to act casual. I haven't told Anna I bumped into him. I forgot, I think, because of all the school stuff.

"I am familiar with the concept of him, yes," says Anna, pulling out a pen and adding *EYELINER* on the bottom of her list.

"I bumped into him the other day when I was out with Mabel."

There's a silence as Anna puts her pen back in the little pencil case she has in her bag, zips it up, and then looks at me. She cocks her head to one side, curls a lock of orange hair around her finger, and says, "Spill."

"He crashed his bike. I was awkward. He was covered in mud. There's not that much to tell."

"What did he say? Did he like Mabel? Was he nice? Did you chat?"

"He asked if I'd had sarcasm flakes for breakfast."

"Ooooh." Anna scrunches up her mouth to one side, the way she does when she's thinking. "But *how* did he say it?"

I think about Gabe, dripping with mud, and me, standing there with a recalcitrant Mabel on the end of her reins. "Just like a question?" I say, but I'm not really sure. He might have been joking. God, it's hard having my brain sometimes.

"Interesting . . ." says Anna. "He might be at Charlotte's party."

She waggles her eyebrows suggestively at me, and taps her front teeth with the lid of her pen.

We finish up our drinks and head out onto Chapel Street.

∘∘∘

I'm going a bit giddy from being in Boots, where the lights are super shiny and there's so much stuff everywhere. There are rows and rows of lipsticks and signs that are screaming and the clatter of people putting their baskets on the counter and the smells of perfume and nail polish being sneakily tried out by girls from Leah's grade. And old people bumbling around with baskets over their arms getting in the way and it's all just so LOUD.

My brain is end-of-term tired. We couldn't stop giggling in English this morning and the whole class almost ended up with an after-school detention. I reckon the only reason she didn't do it was Mrs. Markham wanted the holidays to come almost as much as we did. She flew out of the classroom even faster than us when the final bell went.

I've got a gift token left over from my birthday and Mum's given us some money-off vouchers she had in her purse. We chuck everything in the basket and spin around the shop, laughing at nothing and everything until we clatter down the hair-dye section and bump straight into Holly Bloody Carmichael, who is leaning casually against the posh makeup counter, twirling a lock of her streaky blond hair and talking to—

"Eek," says Anna unnecessarily.

I try to hit reverse gear, but I end up stepping backward onto her foot, so she wobbles sideways. With a crash, a cardboard display of mascara falls off the shelf. Holly looks across at us, her lip curling slightly. Gabe Kowalski, standing in the middle of the shop with a basket full of baby food, raises an eyebrow as if to suggest that we are completely inept specimens of humanity who probably shouldn't be allowed out without our parents supervising us.

"Er. Hi." I do a flapping sort of wave thing, like an ailing sea lion.

"And bye." Anna pulls me by the arm back out of sight and down toward the tills.

"Oh my God."

She's owl-eyed.

"D'you think they're—" She stops midsentence as the woman behind the counter takes the basket and bleeps everything through the till.

We don't speak again until we're outside the shop and heading for Primark, where I've seen black fake nails that'll cover my half-chewed stumpy end-of-finger disasters.

"Together?" I finish her sentence. "No, I reckon they were just talking."

"God, I hope so. He seems nice. It would be a shame if he ended up with Holly."

I feel a lurch of dread about tomorrow night. It's weird how you can be so excited about something and at the same time utterly sick to the stomach. "You don't think Charlotte's invited Holly and her lot, do you?"

Anna shakes her head vehemently. "No chance. Her mum had final say over the invites, and she doesn't approve of them."

I've found the fake nails and we're turning to pay for them when I spot the PERFECT thing to wear tomorrow. I start making my way through the sea of clothes racks. It's getting to the point where I'm a bit seasick from shop-ness, but I just want to get to it and pay and then we can leave. I pull the T-shirt off the rail and turn to Anna, holding it up against myself, pulling a silly face.

"TARDIS!" Anna squeals.

"I *know*." I beam at her because she gets it instantly. Never mind My Little Pony, this is it.

"Seriously? A *Doctor Who* T-shirt? How old are you?"

I spin around to locate the voice.

Holly, who appears to have taken on a new role as our stalker, is standing behind me with her arms folded across her chest. I spot Emma and Lucy, her foot soldiers, rifling through the sale rack, which is full of lurid skinny-fit Lycra stuff.

I hold on to the T-shirt awkwardly. The coat hanger is sticking into my collarbone because I've still got it pressed up against my chest. I can feel myself going beetroot red all over, but I just stand there while Holly looks at us, Anna with her arms full of shopping bags and me with a TARDIS draped across me like some kind of Primark toga. Eventually, after about fifteen minutes or five seconds—I can't quite tell—she stalks off, cracking chewing gum as she leaves.

"Well, I think it's nice," says Anna, giving a little nod of defiance. "And sod her. She's just jealous because we're invited and she's not."

ooo

I leave Anna at the end of Chapel Street and head down the road toward home. It's weirdly warm, because the Indian summer they promised has arrived. On days like this I love living here. In the middle of summer when it's heaving with holiday tourists and you can't walk down the road without someone's infant waving a sticky paw covered in candy floss at you, not so much. But when autumn comes, we reclaim the town as ours. It might be tattered around the edges, and a bit dodgy in parts, but I like it here. It's familiar. And that works for me. I turn the corner onto our road, and the red of an unfamiliar car flashes through the bushes that grow scruffily over the wall of our drive. We don't know anyone with a red car, and—I can feel my steps slowing almost involuntarily—I can't face people tonight. Not ones I don't know, anyway. I've done town and school, and that's enough.

I creep up the side of the driveway, squeezing past the fire-engine-red car, noticing as I do that it's tidy inside—ours is covered in sweet wrappers and leftover Costa cups, newspapers, and the junk mail Mum opens while she's sitting at traffic lights. This car has nothing in it but a glossy, unopened packet of Marlboro cigarettes on the passenger seat, and it's dust-free and spotless.

"Grace."

I see Leah's distorted face through the glass as she wrenches the front door open from inside. She's already changed into a pair of tartan pajama bottoms and a Batman T-shirt, her hair clipped out of her face, a half-eaten apple in her hand. She looks completely unruffled by the fact that there's *someone* here, and it makes me irrationally cross that she just copes with stuff.

I glare at her and walk past without saying anything, shifting the weight of my bag on my shoulder as I head straight up the stairs. I'm hungry and I want a coffee and there's *conversation* coming from the kitchen, and laughing. I had this part of the day all planned and now it's screwed up and I'm not impressed at all.

"Grace, darling." I can hear Mum calling up the stairs, and there's a tone to her voice I don't quite recognize. "Is that you?"

I don't answer, because obviously it is, given that Leah has skipped back into the kitchen with her perfect-daughter halo gleaming, and who else would be making their way upstairs?

"Grace?" Mum calls again, the same weird edge to her voice.

I dump my bag on the bed.

My bedroom is not tidy. Okay, that's a bit of an understatement. My bedroom is a festering, chaotic, possible health hazard. I can't actually see the carpet because my stuff is all over it, and the bed hasn't been made because—well, I don't have time to make the bed in the morning, and I've banned Mum from her "helpful" tidying expeditions where she starts throwing out stuff I might need and touching everything.

I fish out my jodhpurs from the end of my bed, where they're tangled in the covers, and pull them on under my school skirt, over my tights. I can't be bothered with getting changed properly, so I pull a hoodie over the top of my school shirt and squiggle out of my skirt. It lies on the floor like a deflated gray jellyfish.

My boots are in the kitchen. I'm going to have to face whoever it is.

○○○

"There she is," says Mum, and she's got her *please don't do anything appalling* face on, the one where she looks at me with her nostrils slightly flaring and her eyes popped open just a tiny bit too much, and tries to catch my eye.

I do. Not. Want. To. Look. At. Her.

And I especially don't want to look at The Other Person.

So I don't.

I slide through the gap between her chair back and the wall and capture my boots from the back door.

"Grace," Mum repeats as I pull on my boots, "this is Eve. My friend from university I was talking about the other day?"

"Oh."

Mum does a silly little laugh, one I haven't ever heard her do before, and reaches across the table. She tips some wine into the two glasses that are sitting there. She leans forward and gives one to Eve-from-university, who is sitting, with skinny legs in skinny jeans, and a stripy blue-and-white top and expensive-looking hair. Eve-from-university turns to look at me.

"Hi, Grace. Wow, you look like your mum, don't you?"

I roll my eyes.

Mum gives me The Look. "Grace is just off to the stables, aren't you?" She leans forward, putting her chin in her hand, looking at Eve, who is rifling around in her posh-looking handbag.

"Have a good time, darling. Eve's staying over tonight, as she's working in the area for a while, so we'll try not to keep you up too late misbehaving."

And they laugh loudly, and clink their glasses together, and Eve stands up. She walks across the tiles of the kitchen, as if she has every right to be there, and she opens the top half of the kitchen door, and she leans her body out slightly. Then, looking at Mum, she flips open a cigarette box and pulls one out. She half raises an eyebrow at Mum, who shakes her head almost imperceptibly, eyes wide again. And then Eve lights up, sucking the smoke down deep into her lungs, before turning to blow it back out into the garden.

I leave the room feeling weirdly unsettled, just as Leah is walking back in from the sitting room. Because I feel weird, I sort of shoulder barge her in the doorway so she bangs off, sideways, and yelps angrily. But I don't turn around. I just grab my coat from the post at the end of the stairs, and leave.

CHAPTER SEVEN

"Who pissed in your cornflakes?"

I've crashed down the water buckets from Mabel's stable beside the taps, just as Polly appears out of nowhere.

"Nobody."

"Why're you banging stuff around like you're in a major mood, then?"

I look up at Polly. She's got a hay net over one shoulder and the spikes of her bleached-blond hair have flopped a bit because of the drizzly rain, but she still manages to look good somehow. She's got her ears pierced about ten times and a silver hoop through her eyebrow, which is amazing and something I'd love to do except for (a) unimaginable pain and (b) I would be grounded for all eternity.

I shrug. And I don't know why, because usually I'd just say nothing, but my mouth forms the words and they fall out.

"My family is being weird."

Polly gives a sort of upward nod of acknowledgment. "Yeah, they do that."

And I pull an awkward face, which I hope says sorry, because I remember that Polly doesn't speak to her parents anymore. She lives with her girlfriend, Melanie, in a flat above the Spar, because when she told her parents she was gay they threw her out, like something from the 1980s, when everyone was homophobic and ignorant.

Anyway, it's probably not fair to moan about Mum being weird when Polly doesn't see her mum at all, so I shut up and change the subject.

"Are you working tomorrow?"

Polly laughs as Bruce, the huge black thoroughbred who lives in the stable by the taps, reaches over her head and starts hoovering up strands of hay from the net. "Hey, fatso, that's not for you."

Bruce, who was rescued from the slaughterhouse and is an ex-racehorse, is the most athletic thing you've ever seen. He's huge, and spare, and his whole frame ripples with muscles. He moves his big head out of the way and heaves a dramatic sigh.

"Yeah, I'm working all weekend." Polly gives me a look. "You about?"

I shake my head.

"Ohhh. It's The Big Party, isn't it?"

I'm not quite sure how she manages to give it capital letters, or how Polly even remembers me telling her about it the other week when we were raking up leaves, but—

"Yes."

I always get weirdly formal when I have to ask someone a favor. It's like I lose the power of speech.

"I was wondering if you could possibly look after Mabel for me?"

"No chance." Polly gives a flat shake of her head, her mouth a straight line.

I feel a swoop of sick panic. Mum said she's going out with Eve, so there's no way she'll be up for getting covered in horsehair and hay. I need someone to check Mabel at teatime and Anna's supposed to be getting ready at mine and there's no way I can be in two places at once and—

"Course I will." Polly grins. "I was teasing, silly."

I shake my head and put on a smile. I like Polly, because she's cool and interesting and nice. And she knows everything there is to know about horses. Although sometimes she makes me feel a bit on edge, because I never quite know if she's joking or not. But I'm getting better at guessing.

ooo

"She's looking good," Polly calls, climbing onto the gate by the outdoor school. It's a bit later and I'm circling Mabel around, cantering her so slowly that it's like sitting on a rocking horse.

"Give a little bit with that outside rein, and push on with the inside leg a bit, get her reaching underneath a bit more."

I do what Polly says and suddenly it's as if we've been powered up and we're soaring, seahorses on waves, and it's amazing. I circle her again and then let Mabel fly around the long side of the school, letting her reach out, her mane floating in the air, before gathering her to a halt in front of the gate. All the stress I felt earlier has disappeared. If I could live here at the stables, I'd be quite happy.

Polly reaches out and smooths Mabel's forelock. I can see Melanie making her way down the track. She's still wearing her office-y work clothes and skirting the puddles in sensible-looking shoes, which look weird when I'm used to seeing her in her roller-derby team T-shirts, and shorts with stripy tights. She puts a finger to her lips, and so I don't say a word as Polly reaches into her pocket, finding a mint for Mabel to eat as a reward for working hard. Mabel gives a chuntering little noise of happiness as she crunches, shaking her head up and down so that the clinking noise of her bridle disguises Melanie's footsteps.

"Gotcha."

Polly gives a squeak of delight as her girlfriend grabs her around the waist from behind and squishes her hello. She turns, grinning.

"Thought you were going straight to training?"

"Nah." Melanie takes the mints from Polly's hand and helps herself to one, offering me up the packet. I shake my head.

"Jamie said I could get off a bit early," Melanie says through a mouthful of mint, "so I thought I'd see if you wanted to come along and do penalty timing for scrimmage?"

Polly screws up her face, looking down at her filthy jodhpurs.

"Like this?"

Melanie laughs. "It's derby, Poll."

When I'm eighteen, I'm going to do roller derby. Anna and I went to watch Melanie in a bout once and it was the most amazing thing. Everyone was so nice and friendly and they've got cool clothes and it's like being in the best gang ever, as far as I can see. Plus roller skates—and tattoos and blue hair and—

"I need to check the stables. There isn't time."

Polly looks like she'd like to go. It occurs to me then that I could offer.

"I'll do it, if you like?"

Polly and Melanie both beam at me, and I feel a sense of getting it right wash over me like a lovely wave. It's hard to explain. Learning this stuff—what makes people happy—it's like dealing with Mum. I've already worked out that if I act all charming and lovely with her, and don't argue back, I can pretty much do what I like. Sometimes I think people are weird. *Most* of the time I think people are weird. Or maybe they just know this stuff instinctively. I feel like I'm putting the world together in pieces.

"Grace, you're a star." Polly jumps down from the gate. "Just make sure everyone's got hay and water, and I'll do Mabel for you tomorrow night."

"Oh yeah," says Melanie. "Hot date?"

I can feel myself going scarlet-cheeked and I look down at Mabel's neck, flipping over a stray piece of her mane from one side to the other.

"Big party," Polly says.

"Ah," says Melanie, as if those two words explain everything.

Polly gives Mabel a last rub on the forehead and looks up at me for a moment. "Just don't stress about it, okay? You're cool, Grace."

"God," says Melanie, rolling her eyes. "I wouldn't be fifteen again if you paid me."

ooo

I've checked the horses and made sure all the stable doors are bolted shut. Okay, I've triple-checked, because I was a bit stressed about someone getting out in the middle of the night and Polly getting into trouble for leaving me to lock up. And Mabel is in her stable on a bed of snowy-white wood shavings, which smell so delicious that I'd quite like to lie there for the night and not go home. Her stable and all her stuff are always immaculate—Mum always comments that if I could keep my bedroom like that, blah blah blah, but—I shudder for a second, remembering that back home *she* is probably still there.

Eve.

Making the kitchen feel all weird and unsettling, and Mum doing that fake-sounding laugh and acting like someone else.

It's supposed to be my safe place, but I don't want to go home.

CHAPTER EIGHT

"Here you are, you two."

Anna's mum is carrying a plate of dips and tortilla chips, but they're sort of floating in midair because there's nowhere to put them. She raises her eyebrows at the state of Anna's room.

"Hang on." Anna sweeps a space clear on her dressing table, and a tsunami of eyeliner pencils and hairspray cans and Pringles tubes swooshes over the side, landing on the carpet.

"Anna, this place is atrocious. You're not going to Charlotte's party until it's sorted." She gives me a smile. "I bet your room doesn't look like this, does it, Grace?"

"You're joking, Mother?" Anna snorts with laughter. "Grace's room is a health hazard. There was something *growing* in a cup under her bed."

At home this morning, I'd decided that the best thing to do was to stay out of the way. Mum was grumpy and hoovering the stairs when I left the house earlier, and Leah was on the phone as usual. So I texted

Anna and we agreed that the party (The Party. Oh God, it's here . . .) was going to need an intensive all-day getting-ready session.

So we're here now, fixing nails and trying to work out how to clip blue hair-extension things onto the back of Anna's head, and her mum's going to take us up to Charlotte's at seven thirty, and—I close my eyes at this bit because it makes me feel sick—we're supposed to stay over. I don't want to stay over. In fact, if I think about it, I can feel the knot in my stomach getting bigger and lumpier and I know I'm not going to be able to sleep all night in Charlotte's house.

"Is anyone else sleeping over besides us?"

I try to make my voice sound casual. Anna and Charlotte's mothers have concocted this wonderful plan between them and I'm too polite to say no, even though it's making me feel sick. I like routine and knowing what's happening and everything being the way I organize it and most definitely not surprises like this.

Anna half turns from the mirror, her mouth half-open, one finger still pulling her eyebrow where she's trying to tweeze away completely invisible stray hairs.

"No, just us." She puts down the tweezers for a second. "I've no idea what Mum was thinking when she agreed with Charlotte's mum that it'd be easier for us to stay over."

"Probably that she wouldn't have to get up at one in the morning to come and pick us up?" I know it makes sense, but butterflies in my stomach are now stomping around in gigantic work boots.

"Yeah, and she can have a glass of wine and some *quality time* with Dad." Anna rolls her eyes before turning back to look at her reflection.

"Does she realize we don't actually get on with Charlotte?"

"She's a parent." Anna drops the tweezers onto the carpet before turning around to show me her new and improved (can't actually see any difference, but we won't mention that) eyebrows. "She doesn't think."

I take a deep breath. We're sharing a room—it'll be fine—and Mum's already texted to say that if I get stressed out she'll come and get me. She followed that text with another, which said *except I'm going out to the cinema with Eve, so if you could try to have fun, darling, that'd be lovely.* So we all know where we stand, really.

"So Polly's looking after Mabel?"

Anna's scrolling through her phone, which is basically crammed with a million updates about tonight.

I nod. I'm sitting cross-legged on Anna's bed in pajamas because I don't want to put my party stuff on yet. I know if I do I'll spill something on it because I'm officially the clumsiest person on the planet—and even more so when I'm stressed out. And I am officially stressed out. I've already gnawed off all the nail glue that I got stuck all over my fingers when I was fixing on the fake black nails earlier.

"D'you think people who wear fake nails all the time just stop noticing them after a while?"

Anna looks at my fingers, and I spread them out for examination. She doesn't bite her nails, so she's painted her own ones purple.

"They look good."

"Yeah, but I couldn't pull my trousers up properly when I went to the bathroom earlier."

"Maybe posh people have professional trouser-puller-uppers?" Anna giggles at this and reaches across, plonking the dips and chips on the bed between us.

"I dunno." I look down at my nails and they look ugly all of a sudden, like I'm trying too hard. And they're making my hands feel claustrophobic.

Breathe, breathe.

Tonight is going to be good.

I remember Polly's words. *You're cool, Grace.*

All I have to do is remember to be cool.

ooo

I don't even have time to let the gigantic wave of utter terror hit me when we arrive at Charlotte's farmhouse, because the music is already banging out of the barn so loudly that my brain stops working properly and I'm lost.

It's dark outside and the doors are covered with twinkling fairy lights and there's a fire pit on the terrace that wraps around the front of the house, which has warm light glowing from all the windows. And I remember that behind one of those windows is the room where me and Anna have to sleep tonight, when I can't escape to my own bed and my own things and the safety of rolling myself up like a burrito in a blanket and—

"Anna, Grace." Charlotte's mum, Lisa, is our GP. She smiles at me with that look that I get from doctors and teachers and people like that, the one that suggests she's always half expecting me to burst into tears or set her dog on fire or something. She waves her arm, motioning us into the house, kissing Anna's mum hello at the same time.

"Girls, if you just head upstairs, your room is the third on the right. Put your bags down and fix your eyeliner or whatever it is you lot do"— she shares a smile with Anna's mum—"and then you can go and *get the party started*." She sings the last bit, which is so completely cringe-makingly awful that Anna and I gallop up the stairs in horror before slamming the door shut and bursting out laughing. Charlotte might have the poshest house and the most expensive sixteenth birthday party on the planet, but her parents are still mortifying. That's sort of comforting, really.

When we were really small, Charlotte and I had a shared birthday party once, because our birthdays are so close together. Mum and Dad and Charlotte's parents hired a hall and a magician. We were supposed to sit alongside him and help him with his act. Charlotte performed beautifully, and I spent the party under the table playing with a castanet that I sneaked out of his music box.

I can't think of anything worse than a gigantic birthday party, apart from a gigantic *surprise* birthday party. I like knowing exactly what my birthday is going to have in it, and that's me, Leah, Mum, Dad, pizza, unlimited Coke refills, and ice cream sundaes afterward. I've done it every birthday since I was four.

Anyway, the room is amazing. It's got two single beds with fat stripy duvets and an en suite bathroom and there's a bottle of mineral water on each bedside table, and magazines. It's like a hotel. Anna and I drop our bags on the floor and we head downstairs.

Charlotte's dad is stacking a load of glasses on a tray in the kitchen. He looks up at us over the top of his glasses, which are slipping down on his sweaty nose, and smiles.

"All right, girls?" He puts the tray down and pushes up his glasses with the back of his arm. "I think a few of them have arrived while you were upstairs. I'll be out to the barn in a minute if you want to head over. Help yourselves to drinks and stuff."

The barn looks like the director from every teen movie you've ever seen has been left in charge of decorations. No wonder Charlotte's such a princess. She lives the life of a Disney Channel character. I'm half expecting everyone to burst into song in a moment just to finish the picture off. Anna looks at me sideways.

"Were you expecting this?"

I shake my head in silent amazement.

"Okay, well, we can officially say that Charlotte has won at parties before it's even started."

There are fairy lights strung from the huge wooden beams, and casually stacked bales of straw divide the whole place up into cozy little minirooms where I can see people from school are already settling in to their usual cliques. I feel my stomach tighten with anxiety, and I'm tapping my fingers against the sides of my thighs because it calms my nerves a bit. The music's so loud I can't hear myself think properly.

If I let this spiral, I could be out of here in two seconds flat, calling Mum out of the cinema and telling her I want to be back home, where everything is safe. I put my hand into my pocket, feeling the comfortable rectangle of my phone, when I remember.

She's at the cinema with Eve, so she wouldn't even get my text. And when we stopped by to collect my purse, which I'd forgotten, Mum was distracted and answered the door with her hair half-dry and a brush in her hand. And Leah, who was supposed to be going for a sleepover with Malia, had been weirdly dressed up with a ton of makeup on and when I asked her why she'd been slidey-eyed and didn't answer.

"Anna, Grace, there you are."

Charlotte, holding two glasses with something pink in them, smiles at us as if we're her long-lost relatives. I look back at her, realizing that I'm frowning when Anna gives me a slight shove with her elbow.

"What?" I look at her sideways.

Anna widens her eyes and shakes her head almost invisibly.

"*So* glad you could make it," continues Charlotte, sounding weirdly like she's been taking etiquette lessons, and also like she's about forty-five. "Dad made some fruit punch. Don't tell, but I've sneaked in a little something." She gives a little smile and taps the side of her nose. "Now, if you need anything at all, just shout, and have a wonderful time."

Charlotte's dad appears as we're standing by the side of the barn, taking our first mouthfuls of the punch. It tastes sort of strawberry-ish, but when it's going down it gives a whoosh of something else in my throat and it makes me cough.

"Now, I know what you teenagers are like," Charlotte's dad says, smiling, "so I got you a little something." He motions to the big old trestle table behind us, which is laid out with neatly stacked bottles of beer and cider. "Nothing too strong, not enough for anyone to get into any mischief—"

"Dad," says Charlotte, actually blushing, which makes her look slightly human for once. "Honestly, we'll be fine."

And she shoos him out, pulling the barn door behind her. Ed and someone I recognize from the other grade are fiddling with the music, and it drops down to silence for a moment before they've swapped whatever was playing for something on their phone. Charlotte fluffs up her hair and straightens her dress. It's super tight, and appears to be made of the same fabric as Mabel's leg bandages, but I suspect my fashion knowledge might be slightly lacking. She marches across the room to chat with her gang of girlfriends, all of whom are hanging on her every word, nodding their heads and sipping their glasses of punch through straws.

It's all very civilized. In fact, if I'm honest, it's not quite what I expected. Nobody's dancing, the atmosphere is a bit weird—like primary-school Christmas parties, where the hired DJ would come in and play music and nobody would dance until the games started.

"We need Musical Chairs or something."

"We need something to look at, if you ask me," Anna shouts back in my ear. "Where's Gabe?"

"Maybe he's not coming?"

Anna pouts her lower lip and fiddles with the straw in her empty glass. "D'you want some more?"

I feel a bit warm and whooshy inside, the way that a glass of red wine with dinner makes me feel. I don't drink it because it tastes nice (it's like flowery vinegar), but it feels polite to take it.

"Okay."

Anna, with that weird friend-of-the-family confidence thing, marches up to the table where the punch bowl is sitting, and scoops up two glasses full to the brim. She brings them back over. As she's walking, I notice she's started something, and I see Emily and Daisy sidling over and helping themselves to some more too—and we clink the edges of our glasses together.

"Here's to whatever Charlotte put in this." Anna looks at me and downs her drink in one.

And the next half an hour goes by in a weird whirl, which I think must be the punch because suddenly everything seems a bit blurry and

I've been given a bottle of cider by Anna and we're laughing about nothing and Charlotte's parents have come in for what they promise is their last *we're just checking everyone's okay* check. And everyone's still huddled in little groups—we've joined Emily and Daisy and the others. Megan's telling us about her big cousin taking her to Reading Festival during summer vacation—again. We're all listening politely and nodding in the right places—well, Anna is; I'm half watching the door and wondering why Gabe and his friends aren't here, and I can see Charlotte is too, when there's a crash and the door bursts open.

Charlotte's Great Dane lollops into the room and launches himself at one of the tables on our side of the barn, which is covered with a cotton tablecloth. Somehow he manages to shove it out of the way, and with his gigantic paws spread, he shoves his face into the neatly arranged party food, which lies underneath.

"HAMISH!"

Charlotte's mum is so loud she blasts over the music, which is pretty impressive.

"Mum!" Charlotte's hands are on her hips and her sweet hostess-of-the-year expression has been replaced with utter fury. "I TOLD you not to let him in here."

"I didn't!" Charlotte's mum pants with the effort of hauling Hamish off the table. Hamish, undeterred, turns his head sideways and takes a massive bite of birthday cake.

"You absolute *pig*," shouts Charlotte at Hamish, who has a birthday candle sticking out of his mouth like a cigarette. "Out!"

Hamish, looking unimpressed, licking his lips, is dragged away from the table and toward the door and certain disgrace.

"Gabe!" Charlotte's eyes light up as—just in time to save the day—he saunters in, late, accompanied by his best friends Archie and Jacob, and followed by—

"Holly?"

The music is banging and the lights are dim and Charlotte's mum is too busy extracting a disappointed Great Dane out of the room to notice that Gabe's brought a plus one. And a plus one who was categorically Not Invited.

Charlotte's face manages to register delight and fury in the space of about five seconds. She whirls around on her heel and gathers four glasses, tipping the last of the punch into them before turning around again, placing stripy paper straws in three of them.

"Nice T-shirt," says Holly to me as she passes, pulling a face. I look down at my feet.

"Sorry, I'm out of straws," says Charlotte icily. "We had just the right amount, you see."

I open my mouth to say that, no, there's another packet on the table over there, and then I realize that Charlotte's making a point. But I can tell that that's the lamest excuse ever, and Holly doesn't even let it register. She just takes the strawless glass, downs it in one, and takes a flat bottle of something clear out of her bag.

"Sausage rolls. Excellent," says Archie, helping himself to four at once.

I don't really know how things happened. It's like time kaleidoscoped and one minute they'd all arrived and the next—because, weirdly, Gabe has this effect on people—we were messing around and actually goofing off, playing Musical Chairs and laughing our heads off and it was childish and silly and brilliant and everyone was laughing. I suppose the cider helped. And I wasn't even superglued to Anna's side, which is what usually happens. She was off somewhere else and I was hanging out like an actual *look at me, I'm doing this properly* proper person.

"Just going to the loo," I say, leaving the girls, who are covered with straw after someone broke open one of the bales and we ended up having a straw fight, throwing it around until the barn was carpeted with the stuff and the room smelled all deliciously soft and warm and like a stable and I felt safe.

"All right, Grace?"

I can see shapes by the fire pit, but they're in shadow.

"Hi."

I can't see who it is and suddenly I feel awkward again, like I'm failing the how-to-do-this-right test. So I keep walking toward the house and the bathroom.

My eyeliner has smudged and I've got straw in my hair. The light in the bathroom is yellow-bright, and my eyes look a bit mad and red and wild and I know if Mum were here she'd be giving me That Look, the one that says it's time to calm down now, darling, but I don't want to because I feel almost dizzy with the everything of it all.

I go back outside and the shadow people are still there, and I make my way over. It's Emily, with Archie, Tom Higginson of two-broken-ankles fame, Megan, and—with a sort of internal sigh of familiarity and relief, I realize—Anna.

There's a click and a flare of light, which illuminates Tom's face. He inhales on a cigarette and passes it toward me, eyebrows raised, his mouth pursed as if he's holding his breath.

"I don't smoke, thank you," I say, watching as he exhales a stream of green-smelling smoke, which swirls through the air. He gives a satisfied nod, and looks at me with an odd expression I don't recognize. I look at Anna, whose eyes widen slightly, but she doesn't say anything. He offers her the cigarette and she shakes her head.

"I'm all right, thanks."

I feel like I've missed something again. Anna seems to know what the right thing to say is, because nobody looks at her like she's weird.

Archie reaches across and takes it between finger and thumb, sucking smoke into his lungs, his eyes narrowed.

"I'll have some," says Megan.

"I'll see you inside," I say to nobody in particular, and I make my way back to the barn.

I've screwed up somehow and because I'm already teetering on the edge it's as if all the magic shatters out of the evening. My bones ache with tiredness and my head is crashing full of noise and the people are everywhere and I want it all to stop now, but when I look at my phone I see it's midnight and there's a text from Leah that says—

If Mum asks, I was at Malia's house this evening, okay?

—which doesn't make sense because obviously she was at Malia's house, because that's where she said she was going, and I want a cup of coffee and bed and—

"Grace!" Rhiannon drags me by the arm into the center of the room, where there's a big circle of people sitting on the straw-covered floor. "Come on, we're playing Spin the Bottle."

It feels as if everything in my vision is beginning to melt. The music is banging and the voices are going wonky and everything feels as if it's been smudged, as if someone took an oil painting and smeared it sideways with the palm of their hand.

"You okay?"

Anna appears out of nowhere and sits down beside me. She's cross-legged and she sort of bobs herself sideways, giving me a shoulder nudge, which is comfortingly familiar because it's her, and because it reminds me of Mabel. The room smells of beer and too many perfumes and hot people and squashed sausage rolls.

"I'm not sure I'm exactly a Spin the Bottle sort of person," I say to Anna.

"You'll be fine," says Anna, and for the first time since I can remember, I worry that I'm a sort of awkward inconvenience. And she's like a sort of talisman, and I don't want to risk that. She keeps me safe. So I just sit there on the floor.

I'm feeling really weird now. I could just get up and leave, except I'm sort of jammed in between people and it would be super awkward and maybe I could just escape when nobody is looking, which isn't now.

I try to distract myself. I watch as Holly positions herself directly opposite Gabe, and Charlotte edges herself in beside him, smiling at him sweetly. She looks a bit fuzzy around the edges and she's got a bottle of cider, which she's drinking through a straw. ("Do we assume they hadn't run out after all?" Anna whispers to me.)

Her makeup is still perfect, though. How do people *do* that?

"Right then, everyone," says Holly loudly. The circle listens, because Holly's like that. Charlotte looks unimpressed.

Gabe, who's joking with the boy sitting next to him, doesn't pay any attention to Holly.

Someone turns the music down, which helps my head a bit, but the jostling noise of everyone is so *loud* that I want them all to just stop talking, now. I want to scream at them to shut up. I start picking at the fake black nails, pinging them off one by one. It hurts a bit, like I'm pulling the ends of my fingers off, but it distracts me from what's going on, until Anna nudges me again.

"Grace."

I look up from the little nest of fingernails that sits between my crossed legs, and feel myself going ice-cold.

There's a noise, and it's building.

It's a roaring, jeering, cheering sort of noise.

And it's directed at me.

"Come on, then," says Gabe, standing over me.

He extends a hand downward, offering to pull me out of my space in the circle. I shake my head slightly and push myself up. The nails skitter onto the floor and lie on their backs like ten little beetles.

And then the clapping starts, slowly.

Charlotte, who has somehow taken back the hostess role, is standing by a side door that leads out of the barn—not to the terrace, where the fire pit is smoldering, but into a little room with concrete walls and stainless steel sinks. It looks like some kind of milking parlor. Gabe steps back.

"After you."

For a moment I wonder if I could make a run for it, but I'd have to climb across a heaving circle before I made it out of the door.

So I walk into the room, and Gabe follows, and the door closes behind us.

I close my eyes. I can feel the smooth cold grayness of concrete on my hands, which are balled up behind my back and pressing up against the wall, which I'm leaning on for support. And it smells of dust and old things and faintly of something clinical, which reminds me of hospitals and headaches. I can hear the party outside and I wonder if Charlotte's standing right by the door waiting to hear kissing noises, except kissing doesn't make a noise, and this room is mainly just quiet and I realize something in my ears is rushing in the space where the music used to be. I close my eyes and bite the inside of my lip and I realize I'm counting breaths, in out in out in, and I know that I should have gone home ages ago because now I've had enough of all this and there's no way of leaving and I don't know how to say I want to go and . . .

"David Tennant's my Doctor."

I open my eyes.

"What did you say?"

"He's my Doctor." Gabe's voice sounds loud in the echoey concreteness.

He nods his head toward the picture on my T-shirt.

"Ten," he says, explaining unnecessarily, because of course I know what he means. David Tennant's *my* Doctor too, just like Peter Davison is my dad's. And he's peering around the side of the TARDIS on the front of my shirt, with his sonic screwdriver in hand and his long brown dust coat and his Converse.

"I like it."

"Good."

I swallow, and it's so loud that I swear I hear it echo around the whole room.

"It's a bit mental out there, isn't it?"

And I look at Gabe then.

Not Gabe the boy everyone likes from our grade, but Gabe the actual person. And I watch as he runs a hand through his hair, and he does a sort-of smile at me, and I see his one tooth crossed over the other, and then he hitches himself up onto the work surface beside me so he's close enough for me to feel the heat of him through his shirt, radiating toward my arm. And I think then that my heart is thudding so loudly that he can probably hear it and I feel like I'm made of shivers.

And I know why we're in here. The rules say we have to kiss, because it's Spin the Bottle and that's the whole idea. And generally I'm really good with rules because they make life nice and uncomplicated and also *hello*, autism. Duh. We're good on rules. But this is Gabe Kowalski and I am me, so that's not going to happen. I decide to be practical.

"The rules are that we're supposed to kiss."

Gabe's eyes widen slightly.

He's got really, really long eyelashes.

"But it's okay, because we don't have to. Nobody will know."

And then he looks at me for a second that lasts a really long time. And then he sort of cocks his head to one side slightly as if he's thinking about something. And he sort of leans toward me, so the words are almost a whisper on my skin and not an actual sound.

"What if we want to?"

CHAPTER NINE

"An actual proper kiss?" Anna skips sideways beside me as I push the wheelbarrow across the stable yard. We've had this conversation about five times already. The thing is, Anna is desperate to keep the feeling of the party going, and I don't have the words to tell her that I need to switch my brain off. It happens.

People—even the best kind, like Anna—don't really get that I need downtime. But I was on high alert in the lead-up to the party, and even sleeping in a strange bed meant that there were loads of new sounds and smells and noises to deal with, and the people and the—well, the everything. Not to mention the *actual proper kiss*.

I need to be quiet somewhere and just let myself settle, like a snow globe. But it's hard to make people understand that.

So I sort of brace myself and just get on with it, like I'm balancing on a high wire with a basket on my head. Someone ends up adding another thing to the basket, and I can't form the words to say no, so I just grit my teeth. The thing is, I love Anna, so I want to be with her.

She's beside me in a pair of borrowed jodhpurs and my old wellies, skipping with excitement, clueless about what she's supposed to be doing. The wheelbarrow wobbles sideways. It's heavy, and I'm tired, and the acrid ammonia smell is biting at my nostrils. The cold of the metal in my hands is familiar, though, and comfortable. Anna is chattering away and I don't think she even realizes I'm not listening. Last night used up everything I have, and even my brain is tired.

Despite all that, though, I can feel a weird swooping feeling inside when I think about it, so I turn to her and say yes.

"An actual proper kiss."

I feel the nerves kicking in again. It's like someone's shooting electric shocks down my legs and I can hear my heart thumping in my ears. Because when I think about the feeling when I walked out of the room, and everyone was looking at me and Gabe, it felt as if something secret and magical instantly flipped over to a dark side of something dark and horrible and unnerving. Holly Carmichael had said, loud enough that I could hear as I walked past, "Probably the only time freaky Grace will get a snog between now and when she's about thirty," and I'd felt myself go all prickly with embarrassment.

I hadn't looked Gabe in the eye all through the rest of the game. I just looked at the floor and fiddled with a piece of straw, and felt my cheeks prickling with a scarlet that didn't stop. Anna took great pleasure in nudging me every time that Holly didn't get chosen, right up until Charlotte's parents had appeared at one a.m. and their huge driveway was filled with car headlights and parents looking bleary-eyed in the darkness and—in what felt like moments—the spell was broken and the party was over.

I dump the wheelbarrow contents by the muck heap and start forking it up to the top of the steaming pile.

"Eww," says Anna, wrinkling her nose. "Do you have to do this bit?"

I pause for a second, the metal of the fork tines scraping on the concrete. When I'm tired like this, everything is sharper and louder and harder. I don't mind mucking out stables. In fact, I quite like it. I like the way that every day at the stables is the same. I think that won't make sense to Anna, though, because who would like shoveling horse shit?

"Nearly done," I say, because I think that's what she wants to hear, and—feeling guilty—I sort of shove the last bit into the edges with my boot.

"Can we get a coffee now, then?" Anna's walking backward beside me as I trundle the barrow back up and put it in place. She gives a twirl, crashing into the rake and knocking it over with a clatter.

Polly emerges from her horse Hector's stable next door.

"You lot making enough noise?"

Anna, who is a bit nervous around Polly, flushes pink and steps back again, knocking against a shovel, which sets off a domino effect until all the yard tools are lying in a heap on the floor.

"Sorry," she says, trying to gather them up.

Hector, who is a huge bay dressage horse with Bambi eyes, pops his head out of the stable door to see what all the fuss is about. He's got strands of hay hanging from his mouth and he gives a sigh, as if to suggest that we're interfering with his weekend, and disappears back inside.

"When you've quite finished," says Polly, who is definitely joking—she's like a one-person sarcasm-training school, "if someone's putting the kettle on, I'd love one. I'm dying of thirst here."

ooo

"So what happened last night?"

I'm curled up on the sofa in the tack room, surrounded by the smell of saddle soap and leather, with warm, stinky stable rugs hanging overhead. I could live here quite happily. In proper winter, when it gets cold, Jill, who owns the stables, sometimes lights a fire and then I think I could stay forever.

Polly is warming her hands on a mug of coffee, and Anna is perched on the arm of the chair. She flicks me a sideways look.

"I saw that," says Polly. She takes off her beanie hat, rubs her white-blond hair. When it's squashed flat like that, she looks younger. Less spiky, somehow.

And I let Anna tell the whole story, because she's still bursting with it, and I'm on the verge of running out of words. I can feel my batteries going flat, because I've had to negotiate people this morning when usually I just potter around the yard and it's my safe place. The thing is that it sort of feels as if it's not my story now, anyway. It's something that happened in a tiny little bubble, and nobody is ever going to know about it—well, besides me and Anna and now Polly—and normal service will resume at school next week. I'll be Grace, who is on the periphery of things, and Anna will be Anna, who is accepted by the cool people and the nerds and everyone in between, but chooses to be friends with me, and Gabe will carry on being the boy everyone likes, and—

Polly pokes me with the toe of her boot, stretching out her leg.

"So are you going to see him again?"

"Hardly," I say, giving her A Look.

"Well, he kissed you. That suggests an element of interest." Polly cocks her head sideways, looking at me directly.

I look down at the knees of my jodhpurs, which are pretty disgusting, even by my standards. She carries on.

"You like him, right?"

"I don't know him," I say reasonably.

"*Grace,*" says Anna, snorting. "This is Gabe Kowalski we're talking about."

"Okay," says Polly, and I see her and Anna exchanging glances. "So you are physically attracted to him. And kissing him was not an unpleasant experience."

I feel myself go icy hot and cold all over in a rush. No, it was not unpleasant. It was so not-unpleasant that I even forgot that it was happening and I kissed him back and didn't accidentally lick his nose or bang teeth or fall over or any other horrors, which, frankly, wouldn't be that unsurprising given my track record for doing ridiculous things when under pressure.

"Grace?" Anna reminds me that meanwhile, back on planet Earth, they're waiting for an answer.

"I'll *see* him next Monday, I imagine, when we go back to school."

Polly shakes her head, then tears open a packet of Oreos.

"You girls need to take the power back." She stuffs a cookie in her mouth, whole, and continues through a muffle of crumbs. "If you're interested in him, why don't you ask *him* out?"

I don't even know where to start with this one, so I just drink my coffee and pull a face and Anna doesn't say anything either. Polly picks up an old edition of *Horse & Hound* and starts looking at the back pages, and we all sit there in a silence that might be awkward but might not be. I can never quite tell.

It's nothing to do with Gabe being a boy that stops me contacting him. It's just—being me. I don't imagine Polly hesitated for a second before asking Melanie out either. She's just the sort of person who does things. I'm the sort of person who thinks about doing things, then goes home and eats toast instead. Not just that, but the potential mortification factor is so high that it's off the scale. Holly Carmichael has already got me in her sights, and the rumor mill's so efficient at school that I'm already feeling sick at the thought of going back next Monday.

"Is she always like that?" Anna whispers later, from over the top of Mabel's back. We're in the stable and she's tucked up for the night— Mabel, that is, not Anna—and we're waiting for Mum to come and pick us up.

"Polly?" I whisper back. "Yes."

"I want to be like her when I grow up." Anna fiddles with a fluffy piece of hair at the end of Mabel's mane. She's not much good with horses, but she likes Mabel.

"Me too," I say, but I know that the chances of it ever happening are nonexistent. I'm too busy balancing and trying to work out what everyone else is doing and saying and thinking to be able to be my own person like Polly.

Sometimes I think I don't even know who my own person is.

∘∘∘

Thank God there's no Eve when I get back. We've dropped off Anna (I'm slightly worried my spare jodhpurs will be fumigated by her mother and might never make it back to my house, but I'm trying to be Zen about it) and I am super tired and I feel all spacey, like my feet aren't quite making contact with the floor.

The kitchen's all messy, which is weird, because usually Mum's stressing about everything being put away at this time of day and us pulling together and all that stuff. I pull out the dishwasher rack to find a clean bowl, but it's dirty, and full, and nobody's switched it on. I tip a heap of cornflakes into a plastic mixing bowl—it's roughly the same size and shape, and there's nothing else—and pour the last of the milk on top.

The kitchen table is spread with coffee cups and a half-unwrapped copy of the Sunday newspaper. I suspect I've missed today's Eve visitation, and for that I am glad.

"So," says Leah when I walk into the sitting room to find my laptop, "how was the party?"

She's sitting there with a bowl of cereal watching the Disney Channel with her hair in a ponytail and she looks about nine. The fire's lit and it's all warm in there and I'm tempted to stay, but I've reached the point where the noises in the house have separated and I can hear each one individually. And at the same time I can hear them all together—it's hard to explain. It's like I'm trying to process what's going on and I can't filter anything and I can't think at all.

"Okay," I say. And Leah opens her mouth to ask more, and I feel guilty because I get the feeling as I pull the door shut that she looks like she wants to talk, but I can't. I just can't.

"Grace, honey," says Mum as I'm heading upstairs. "Phone. For you."

She thrusts the handset at me as I'm shaking my head. No, I can't do Grandma on a Sunday night.

I shake my head again and put my hand out, palm toward her, as a no, no. No.

"It's your father," she says, which is a strange way of saying it's Dad.

The line is sort of echoey and he sounds as if he's miles away, which he is.

"Hey, darling," he says, and a moment later a little echo says, "Hey, darling."

"Hi, Dad," I say, and I suddenly feel weirdly homesick even though I'm at home, and it almost knocks me sideways and I shut it down, because I'm too tired to deal with that feeling right now. "Shot any good penguins recently?"

"Polar bears." His echoey echo voice comes back. "Not penguins."

"I know," I say. "It was one of those joke things I hear are popular these days."

And I sit down on the landing halfway up the stairs and listen to him and watch my cornflakes turn into orange mush beside me as he talks about what he's been doing and how he can't wait to get back. It's weird because he sounds as if he wants to be there as much as he wants to be here, and I can understand that feeling. It's how I feel about most things.

I miss him.

"How's home?" he asks.

And I think about how home is. I think about the fact that bloody Eve seems to have imprinted herself everywhere and Mum is weirdly distant and Leah's never off her phone. And the place is untidy and not like it normally is and it feels like a wrinkled sock in your shoe that worries away at you all day, making everything feel not quite right so you can't concentrate on anything properly. And I think about how I miss him being here in the office editing and showing me bits he's done.

"Fine," I say. And then in a few moments I say good-bye and take the phone downstairs to Leah, and I forget to pick up my cornflakes, which lie soggily in their bowl on the landing.

I'm just getting into the bath when I hear my phone beep in the bedroom, and I almost don't answer it. But I know that instead of lying there in the quiet water I'll be wondering who it was, so I wrap myself in a towel and pad through to have a look.

It's a number I don't recognize.

Hi, Grace. Do you fancy going out sometime?

And as I'm standing there looking at the screen wondering if it's a joke, it beeps again.

It's Gabe, btw. :-)

CHAPTER TEN

Even I know that there's something a bit weird about your thirteen-year-old sister being the person who helps you get ready for a first date. Well, if we're being exact, *my* first date. Because this is literally the first time that I have ever been out on a date with another human being.

I haven't told Mum, of course, because (a) oh my God, the mortification, and (b) she would probably have some kind of Grace's First Date photo shoot where she'd insist on taking photos to send to Dad, and yeah, well. Also she's still being weird and living on planet Eve and, considering I'm supposed to be the one who gets obsessed with things, she seems to be pretty much focusing on that and nothing else. When I got up this morning, there were no clean knickers left in my drawer, and I had to go and rootle about in the tumble dryer until I found some.

Anyway, I haven't told Mum, and Leah's promised to keep it secret—and usually I'd think that would last precisely as long as it took for me to start annoying her, at which time she'd blurt it out by "accident" just to piss me off. But Leah's acting a bit weird at the moment, which is either some kind of being-thirteen thing or maybe because she doesn't seem to be friends with her BFF Meg at the moment. Normally in the holidays Meg basically lives here, but she hasn't been around at all, and when Mum asked the other day Leah just shrugged and left the room. And usually Mum would have been chasing after her, hassling to know what was going on, but it's weird. It feels like the whole family is unraveling and nobody seems to have noticed.

I want to know what's going on with Leah and Meg, but I'm too busy stressing about what I'm supposed to *do* on a date. My knowledge so far is basically gleaned from a million books (not helpful) and another million retro '80s films (chances of Gabe turning up in a beaten-up convertible borrowed from his dad: zero), so I'm on my own here.

And, just to make things even better, Anna's parents have taken her to a cottage in the middle of Wales where there's literally no Wi-Fi or cell phone coverage. We had a little farewell ceremony for her phone yesterday in the bedroom. She's promised me that she'll keep it charged and attempt to connect to every single open Wi-Fi network she can find in the whole of the Welsh mountains. (Surely farmers must need to check stuff on the internet?)

"Right." Leah hands me an outfit that isn't my usual jeans-T-shirt-cardigan. "Black dress, cardigan, tights, Doc Martens."

"But what about my Doctor Who T-shirt? I wore that at the party and . . ."

I trail off because Leah is giving me a look that says *NO* very clearly. Well, that, and the fact that she's actually taken the TARDIS T-shirt off the bedroom floor and has balled it up in one hand and hidden it behind her back.

"It's a date, Grace. The idea is you make a bit of an effort."

"Fine."

Sometimes I feel like everyone else was handed a copy of the rules and mine got lost.

○○○

"Hey."

I've walked up to the top of Walnut Street, where we arranged to meet, and Gabe's standing there, wearing the exact same things he was wearing at Saturday night's party, which seems a bit unfair if you ask me. I feel like I should be on top of a Christmas tree in this dress. Admittedly I haven't seen many fairies wearing black dresses with tiny Day of the Dead skull patterns all over them, but I suspect it could be a thing. It *should* be a thing.

"Hello," I say, because when I'm anxious I find it really uncomfortable to say abbreviated words.

Gabe looks at me with his very brown eyes, and smiles with his crossed-over teeth.

"You got here okay, then?"

"Well, actually, I got here ten minutes early," I say. "But I realized that I was going to stand here like a spare part for ten minutes and that would be awkward so I thought I'd walk around the block because that would kill time, but it didn't, it only killed two minutes, so I walked around four other blocks and . . ."

Oh God.

"D'you fancy going to the Botanic Gardens, seeing as it's nice? We can get a coffee or something."

I don't know if Gabe's just naturally polite, or whether he was hoping if he said that I'd shut up, but anyway, I stop talking.

We walk along together, side by side, and there's a silence that you could call companionable except I think it's actually the other one, and I try desperately to come up with things to say. And all I can think of are the classes Mum used to take me to at the center when I was younger, where I was supposed to learn how to be a functioning human being, except the woman who ran them was possibly the weirdest person I've ever met.

"So," Gabe says, and there's a little note of something in his voice that makes me think that maybe he's as nervous as I am, because he sounds a bit odd. "*Doctor Who.*"

And I say, "Yes."

And he says, "So. The big question remains. The Master, or Missy?"

And I say, "Oh God, that's really hard, because John Simm was perfect as the Master, but Missy's so deliciously evil and—"

And that's it. And we talk and talk all the way to the Botanic Gardens, and not just about *Doctor Who* either. We talk about school and how Miss Jones the biology teacher is really Victorian and how obsessed Charlotte was with having the perfect party and about our pets and about living here and then we find the cafe and we get a coffee each and decide to sit outside in the park because it's weirdly nice for the time of year.

And there are lots of old people on all the usual benches around the flower bed bits, and down by the duck pond bit, and so we walk along the path to the huge old oak tree that we used to try to climb when we were smaller, and we make our way through the little path where the rhododendron bushes flap wetly against your face as if they've been saving up for a not-rainy day, and we sit down on the little bench where the rose garden is, where there are no people at all.

I drink my coffee, even though I don't really want it, because I realize in that moment, surrounded by rosebushes and the smell of disintegrating autumn things and the still-damp wood of the bench, that I know what's supposed to happen now, but I don't know how it happens. All I know is that my heart is galloping loudly in my chest and I can feel the warmth of Gabe sitting beside me drinking his coffee and he doesn't smell of wood smoke or toothpaste or any of the things boys in books always smell of. He smells of bluebell-and-lavender fabric softener, and I know that because it's the one I like best. And he smells a bit of shampoo, I notice, as he turns toward me, but I don't recognize that smell. It's not horrible, though.

I've watched loads and loads of films to see how it happens when a girl and a boy kiss for the first time, and what seems to happen is that one of them looks at the other one for a moment and they look away and then they look back and then one of them looks at the other one's mouth, which is the universal signal for I Want to Kiss You, and then it just sort of happens.

Except that when you're fifteen, and even if you're with the boy who everyone in your grade likes, the truth is that you both just sit there drinking your coffee and looking at a small brown bird scraping around in the dead leaves of the flower bed, and then, only then, when you reach down to put your coffee cup on the ground at the same time as he does, your faces sort of collide in a way you can't ever explain afterward and—

Kissing Gabe is like—well, actually, I don't have anything to compare this to. Mainly I'm thinking, YES, at least this means that factually if anyone says "sweet sixteen and never been kissed" I shall be able to contradict them, even if it's in my head, and then I'm thinking about *Pretty in Pink*, when Iona asks Andie, "Does he have *strong lips?*" and I'm wondering if Gabe's constitute *strong lips* because my knees feel a bit dizzy and oh my God tongue in mouth. Tongue. In. Mouth.

I pull back for a moment. Gabe looks at me and does a small smile. And I try to arrange my face into an appropriate shape, because I have this serious resting-bitch-face thing going on, and it wouldn't really be the done thing to be scowling at someone with whom you've just exchanged saliva. (Oh God. Don't think about that. This is no time for science.)

And then he leans toward me again, and takes a strand of my hair, and I sort of recoil backward, because I don't like people touching my hair, and he doesn't seem to notice, because he tucks it behind my ear like someone in a film would do. It's such a film-cliché thing to do that I realize he's just winging it too, and I laugh.

And he says, "What are you laughing at?"

And I reach out, because for a moment it feels as if maybe everyone else doesn't know the rules all that well either, and I watch as my fingers lace between his, and I lean forward this time, and I kiss Gabe Kowalski. And this time I don't think about anything.

CHAPTER ELEVEN

'm flying on happy feet (okay, I might even have done a few skips) up the road to our house feeling like an actual proper person. I've been on a date, nothing disastrous has happened, and today I'm winning at being a human.

That's when I notice the flash of a red car in our driveway. Eve's car. I don't want to have to deal with her today. I feel all the happiness whoosh out of me like someone just stuck a pin in my side. When it goes, it goes so fast.

Suddenly I'm tired—I used every last scrap of lovely, funny, sparkly, entertaining Grace on Gabe, because I wanted to be the good bits of me, and now I need to flop and not talk to humans and be on my own.

I can feel my feet dragging with dread as I walk up the road. Withnail is sitting on the neighbors' wall, and I stop to stroke him, watching as he arches himself up to my hand, wishing I could just curl up out here and be peaceful.

By the time I get to the driveway, it feels as if someone's switched off a light inside me, and all the good stuff that's just happened with Gabe—the *I'll text you later*, the kiss at the end of the road, the silly conversation holding hands as we walked back from the Botanic Gardens—it's like it never existed.

I turn the key in the lock and shove the door open. I don't even bother trying to creep in and avoid her—I live here, so why should I? It stinks of a mixture of her perfume and disgusting stale cigarette smoke, and it chokes in my throat. I can hear the clock ticking loudly in the hall and as I kick my shoes off and they slide under the dresser it's as if the sounds are amplified and they echo in my head, which is full to bursting, and I put my hands over my ears for a moment to try to block it out.

I throw my coat at the banister post and it swings sideways and slumps down onto the floor. I leave it there and stomp into the kitchen. Surprise, surprise—they're sitting at the table and—shock horror—they've got a bottle of wine open.

"Grace, darling, you look nice," says Mum. Her smile looks as if she's baring her teeth, because my vision is going weird.

I don't answer. I open the fridge and there's no orange juice. The milk is sitting out on the counter, which makes me want to be sick. I pick it up and pointedly put it back in the fridge, making a mental note not to drink any of it.

"Honey, are you looking for something to eat?" She's put on that fake, singsong voice again, the one she uses when Eve's here. It's like she's playing at being herself and I want to scream at her. She ought to realize I'm on the edge. Normally, she can tell, but since Eve appeared it's as if she stopped looking.

So I ignore her again. There's no bread in the bread bin, the milk's probably off, there's nothing to eat in the fridge and the kitchen—and, yes, I know: I'm a hypocrite—looks like a shit heap.

I hear Eve saying something quietly to Mum, but I can't quite make it out. And out of nowhere I feel it beginning. It's a heat in my head, and my ears are thrumming with red noise. I can feel my chest rising and falling rapidly and it's weird, because there's a split second where I could probably just stop this, just walk out and not let the meltdown happen. But then it's too late and like a wave it hits and my temper rises and I turn around.

"Have you got something you want to say?" I look at *her*.

"Grace." Mum's tone is warning. "You sound like you need some quiet."

Oh, *now* she gets it. Well, it's too late.

"It's not my place to say anything," begins Eve.

"Well, don't, then." I glare at her.

"But Julia's my friend and I'm not going to sit here and listen to you giving her attitude. She's got enough going on without you making life difficult for her—"

"Eve . . ." Mum shakes her head, her eyes sort of half narrowed. "Leave it. Grace, darling, do you want me to run you a bath? Lavender oil?"

I know what she's trying to do. I don't want to calm down. I don't want to take a deep breath. I don't want to fake being lovely Grace-let's-remember-our-manners. I'm sick of that cow being in our house, and I'm sick of everything being different and I want her to go and I want—

"I don't know how you do it," says Eve quietly, reaching across and putting her hand on Mum's arm. She thinks I can't hear her.

"And *I* don't know what you're doing here," I shout at her, and I slam the glass down on the table so milk sloshes over the sides and leaves a puddle on the wood. "Nobody wants you and Mum's just too polite to say that and you should go because you're just a—"

"I'm here because I was invited."

Why doesn't she just shut up?

"Why don't you just shut up?"

Eve's eyes widen for a second and she turns to look at Mum, and I know what she's expecting. But Mum doesn't say anything, she just sits there looking at me and I realize that I'm double-flapping both my hands in agitation now because I've tipped over from slightly pissed off into Hulk smash meltdown mode and my mouth isn't responsible for what it says because it's like having tunnel vision.

"Seriously." I look at Eve with hatred. "You're a tragic old lush with no life—that's why you're trying to take over Mum's."

Eve opens her mouth, but Mum shakes her head.

"Grace, that's enough. Eve is my friend, and I won't have you talking to her like this."

I can't do any more of this. I look at Mum in her brand-new just-like-Eve Converse and her suddenly different jeans and her identical-to-Eve's stripy top.

"You're tragic, you know that? Trying to pretend you're something you're not. You're as bad as *her*."

As soon as I say it, I feel the heart-thumpy realization that I've gone too far and I've hit a sore point, because Mum sort of crumples a bit and it makes me even more furious because she turns to *her* and I'm left standing there. And I hate her for being so pathetic and needy because I miss Dad too, but you don't see me turning into a clone. And then Leah appears out of nowhere, just in time to do her perfect-child, *I'm so virtuous* act, and the red fury hits me again.

"And you don't even care that this whole house has gone to shit since Dad went away."

"Because he's so bloody perfect—" Eve starts, but Mum shoots her a look and she stops talking.

"Grace—"

I turn to leave the room, sweeping a load of papers off the table and kicking the door. And because she's in the way and she's always so perfect and I hate myself, I shove Leah, hard, so she rebounds back-ward against the wall of the kitchen with a surprised noise and I slam the door and crash upstairs with the noise still ringing in my head. I hate them.

As soon as I shut the door of the bedroom and I slump down against it, blocking it shut, I feel the tears starting. I cry and cry until I've run out and then I just sit there for ages feeling like I'm in a black hole. Eventually, I pick up one of my fidget toys and twiddle with it for a while, and it's calming, but I feel sick with what's happened. And guilty for the things I said—well, to Mum, anyway—I still hate *her*—and it's like I imagine a hangover must feel. Like my face aches with crying and I feel this solid lump of guilt in my chest that stops me breathing properly. I hate this. When I was little, it used to happen all the time. Now I'm older and I know what pushes my buttons I can stop it sometimes. But other times it's like there's a game of Jenga going on in my head and I never know what's going to make everything fall apart.

Later—and I've moved onto the bed, because sitting on the floor was making my legs feel weird—I'm lying down, on top of the covers, trying to work out what to do. I can hear noises downstairs, but nobody's coming to make sure I'm okay—when I was smaller and I felt like this, Mum would try to fix it. But she's too busy with Eve and I'm too humiliated to go downstairs and be forced to apologize. And, anyway, I *do* wish Eve would go away and leave us all alone. But I feel like crap for shoving Leah, who didn't have anything to do with any of it.

As if she's heard me thinking about her, there's a knock on the door and I know who it is.

"I brought you coffee," she says. And an arm holding a cup slides through the gap in the door.

"It's fine," I say through the cushion I've pulled up to cover my face because I don't want to look at her. "You can come in."

She slinks in and puts the cup down on my desk.

"Sorry."

I surprise myself by saying it. Most of the time I find it almost impossible to get the word out. Not because I'm not sorry, but because it's like there's a glass bubble in my mouth stopping the words from forming.

"'S all right," says Leah, and she does a sort of flat-mouthed upside-down smile, which means it's okay. "Mum said to bring the coffee up. She said you needed time to calm down by yourself."

And then she leaves.

I feel like I've been dipped in acid—raw and flayed and sore. I'm so tired that even though I'm drinking the coffee Leah's brought me I'll be asleep in a moment, cocooned under the weight of the blankets I'll wrap around me.

ooo

"Sweetheart?"

I'm not awake, but I am, almost. I feel the weight of Mum sitting down on the edge of the bed, the pressure of the duvet pulled tighter across my legs. I don't move. It's gotten dark outside while I've been sleeping.

"I thought you might be asleep." A hand reaches out and rests on my leg. It's quite comfortable, actually. I lie there with my eyes closed, because even if she thought I was awake there's no way I could look at her. When I feel like this, afterward, I can't look at people. It hurts my eyes.

"Eve's gone back to her hotel. I thought you'd want to know that. And, Gracie, darling . . ." There's a pause, and I hear her sighing. "I'm sorry you felt the way you did—the way you do. I'm trying, you know. It's not easy, doing everything with Daddy gone. And all this change—"

She hardly ever calls him Daddy. I imagine his nice smiling face and his beardy chin and the lump of guilt travels up into my throat and becomes a lump of missing and sadness.

I feel her getting up from the bed and switching on my lava lamps. One, two, three, four, until the room is full of purple and pink and blue and red, which I can see through my eyelids—or can I just imagine it? And there's a rustling as she opens a box and I know just before the scent hits me that she's dropped lavender on the little bowl on the radiator.

She sits down again.

"All I'm trying to do is the right thing, darling. Nobody gives us a rule book when we grow up, you know."

She rubs my leg for a moment then gets up again.

"Love you, darling."

As she's closing the door, I say it. It might have been too quiet for her to hear, but I did say it.

"Love you."

And I think,

I'm sorry.

And then I fall asleep again.

CHAPTER TWELVE

reach under my pillow for my phone.

I don't wake up feeling right the day after a meltdown. It's how I imagine a hangover feels—my head hurts, everything is heavy, and I have to drag my body around like an unwilling participant in a party game. I don't want to have a hangover if this is how they feel. I've got enough trouble with my own head messing me up without adding drink to the equation.

The phone's dead—I remember now that it died when I was on the way home from my time with Gabe, which feels like it happened some time in the last century. I reach under the bed for my charger and realize bloody Leah's stolen it again.

The blank black rectangle in my hands could hold lots of things. Right now I'm not sure I want to switch it on and find out what's inside. Leah, who can't actually breathe unless she's checked her notifications once a second, can't understand why I can take or leave my phone. But the truth is life's noisy enough and my head is full of all the things I have to remember when I'm being a person every day: don't be rude, don't stare, don't look blankly into space when you're not thinking anything, shut down the noises of everyone talking, concentrate, hold it together, don't have a meltdown . . .

Oh God.

I climb out of bed and head downstairs, trying to wish away what happened last night.

"Morning, darling," says Mum, who is still surrounded with papers on the dining table. She looks up from her laptop and smiles at me and I feel relieved that she looks back at the screen and doesn't seem to be planning A Little Chat right now.

I feed Withnail, who tells me he's starving to death. I realize when I hear voices from the sitting room that it's Leah's best friend, Meg, I can hear, and that feels like normal and I like it.

Mum taps away at her laptop for a bit while I sit on the counter beside the toaster, waiting for the kettle to boil.

"Empty that dishwasher for me, Grace, honey?"

More tapping. Because I'm feeling heavy with guilt and horrible things after last night, I do it without even protesting. That's usually Leah's department and I feel quite pleased with myself as I stack plates and put the mugs back on the corner shelf by the sink.

"D'you want tea?"

"Mmm? Yes, lovely, thanks, darling."

I butter the toast—leaving crumbs on the counter because I've not had a complete personality transplant, and Leah's bound to be making some in a bit anyway—and make two cups of tea, placing one on the newspaper next to Mum's laptop.

"Oh, watch out—I need that article," she says, shifting it sideways. "I'm applying for a job, actually," she continues, turning the laptop around to show me.

I realize then that Leah would've asked what she was doing. I always forget to ask the questions that people want to be asked. It's not that I'm not interested (well, quite a lot of the time I'm not *that* interested in where my tutor is going for half term, and stuff like that), but it just doesn't really occur to me to ask because I think if they want to tell me, they'll tell me at the end of the process. That's the bit that confuses me. Why do people tell me their thought processes when they're doing a thing?

"Oh," I say, because I realize I've been standing there for I don't know how long.

"You're okay with that?" Mum's voice sounds a bit . . . surprised or something. I can't quite work it out.

"Yep," I say, mainly because I don't have the brain to look at all the bits of paper and the stuff on the screen that's already giving me the warnings of a flickery headache.

She puts her arm around my waist and pulls me in toward her. She smells of something purple and soft and her hair is fuzzly from the shower.

"Hug?"

And I put my arms around her, because I get the feeling that she's the one that needs one. I don't particularly like hugs when I'm processing other stuff, because it's just another bit of information to deal with, but I know that other people like them, so I do them more than I would otherwise. And right now I'm still feeling bruised from last night and I haven't even begun processing what happened yesterday, but I'm putting that on hold in my head until later because I don't have the space to think about the Gabe stuff right now.

"Have you got my phone charger?" I say into the air. She's still sitting there, squeezing me from the middle like I'm a tube of toothpaste. It makes her let go.

"Nope." She looks automatically at her own phone, which is sitting on the table. "I bet Leah's grabbed yours. She's never away from that phone. I'm going to institute some kind of technology ban, actually."

I step backward because I can already tell where this is going, but it's too late. She's off.

"In fact, we should be having more family time, less screen time."

She shuts her laptop. "Monopoly. Proper bonding time. We don't need your father here to do that sort of thing. In fact, really, we need to get used to it . . ."

I back out of the room while she's still talking, because once she's off it can go on for ages. I can hear her looking in the kitchen dresser for the stack of neglected board games already.

"Did you nick my charger?"

"Morning, Grace," says Leah. She's dressed and her hair's been straightened and then twirled at the ends with some kind of curling machine thingy. She's also wearing a crop top that shows off her tan and makeup that makes her look a lot older than thirteen. If she weren't my sister, I think I'd be a bit nervous of her. She's gone a bit spiky-looking, like she'd fit in with Holly Carmichael's gang quite easily. Meg, on the other hand, has her hair tied back in a ponytail and her usual jeans and sneakers and a hoodie on. She looks like thirteen ought to look. She also looks a bit alarmed, and I get the feeling that she's sort of holding on. It's hard to describe, but it's how I feel all the time and I can always recognize it in other people. Like you're expecting to be caught out at any moment and banished from society.

"Uh, I dunno," says Leah, offhand. "C'mon, Meg, let's go upstairs. I'll do your hair and makeup."

If Meg feels alarmed by this, she doesn't show it.

"Charger?" I repeat.

"Oh," says Leah, and I get this weird feeling that she's trying to look cool in front of Meg, which doesn't make sense because they've been friends since preschool. "It's in the sitting room."

She beckons Meg and they head upstairs.

It's the weirdest feeling. It's like someone shifted everything slightly, and home feels out of sync. Everything's changing and I don't like change.

Maybe a shower will fix my head.

I plug my phone in and leave it behind the sofa.

CHAPTER THIRTEEN

One of the weird things about Really Good Days is you never know when they're going to happen. I'd quite like it if you did, so you could prepare, because I really don't like surprises. Instead, Really Good Days sneak up when you're not looking.

"Grace?" Mum shouts upstairs. "Phone for you."

I lean over the banister and see her standing there, brandishing the landline phone.

"For me?"

"It's Anna."

I gallop downstairs two at a time and grab it from her, closeting myself in Dad's study with my feet curled up underneath me on his office chair.

"Hello. Welcome to 2001." Anna giggles. "You didn't answer the cell phone when I rang it seventy million times, so I thought I'd try the old-fashioned method." She must have found some signal in the depths of Wales. I relax back into my seat, feeling myself smiling. "D'you want the good news or the even better news?"

"Both?" I reply.

"I'm not in Wales." There's a little squeak and a thud, and I suspect Anna is dancing on the spot, wherever she is. "I am HOME. Free. There was some major disaster at the surgery, so Mum had to come back, so I am here and I am freeeeee, and we can do whatever we want for the whole week."

"Stay where you are. I'm on my way over."

"Excellent thinking."

"Give me twenty minutes. Bye." I stand up and make my way toward the door, the sitting room, and my phone, which must now be fully charged.

"Oh, and, Grace?" Just as I am about to end the call, she asks the question. "What happened with Gabe?"

"I'll tell you the whole story when I get there."

"Have you heard from him?"

I unplug the phone from the charger and look at the blank screen. I don't turn it on.

"Um. I don't quite know."

"*Grace . . .*"

ooo

And so I'm walking to Anna's house to escape home because the same-not-same thing is making me feel odd, and the fresh air is making me feel better about what happened last night. Mum's quite happy for me to be out of her hair (I bet she's got That Person coming around again, but I'm not even going to think about that), and she gave me a tenner to go and do something nice. So we're going to the seafront.

I haven't switched my phone on yet, because I've reached the point where I'm feeling a bit like turning it on and seeing a *hi, thanks for yesterday, but see you around* text is not what I want right now. I'm not sure why my brain's decided that's what has happened, but, really, the whole going-out-with-Gabe-Kowalski thing is so unlikely that I've half convinced myself I imagined it, anyway. And I shouldn't be leaping on the phone even if he *has* texted me, because I'm busy doing important things and definitely not thinking about him every five seconds.

(Every ten, perhaps. All right, every five. Or three. But it's ridiculous and I'm a hideous cliché, so now I've agreed with myself that I'll turn the phone on when I get to Anna's house and not before. And her house is right across the other side of town, so that's ages. And I'm thinking about important things like the state of the economy instead.)

This might be a lie.

Because it's sunny and half term, the town is suddenly heaving with people and noise and I've got my headphones in even though I've got no music playing (because of no phone, which I might have mentioned, because of Gabe, which I might also have—SHUT UP, brain). They make the world a bit muffled, which helps when it's busy, because sometimes everything starts to whoosh alarmingly in a way that's like someone turning up and down the volume in my head. And sometimes it whooshes in time with my footsteps, and I look at all the other people going to WHSmith and buying newspapers and coming out of BHS with shopping bags and I wonder if they hear it too. But I don't know how to ask people if their world whooshes, so for now it remains a Great Mystery of Life.

"Jelly beans," I say, patting my pocket when Anna opens the door.

"Excellent," she says, which is why I love her. Because she doesn't say *you need to explain what you're thinking, Grace* and *other people can't read your mind, Grace* and all the other sensible things I've heard a million times from Mum and the therapist at the Jigsaw Center when I was little (before Mum realized that place was hellish, and that forcing me to go there was causing everyone more stress than anything else).

And then she looks at me. And because she knows me too well, she holds out her hand.

"Phone."

"I can't," I say.

"Hand it over," she says.

I don't want to know.

I turn around on the spot while she turns the phone on. If it switches on when I'm on an odd number, I decide, it'll be a good thing, and if I stop on an even number it'll be back to normal, which I realize might actually be quite relaxing because this is all incredibly stressful and I don't think—

(Five.)

"Shall I read it?"

I hold my breath. I shake my head and hold my hand out, take the phone as if it's made of something radioactive (which it is, actually, I think, but even I can see that I'm digressing at this point), and then hand it back again.

"Nope."

"Nope?"

"You do it."

Had a great time last night. Hit me up when you can :-)

Anna reads it aloud, but I can see the words on the screen even though they're upside down.

"Last night?" She raises her eyebrows.

"I'll explain while we're walking," I say.

"That means," she hands the phone back, "call me."

Anna's not being rude. It's just that I'm better with unambiguous, and "hit me up" is a bit vague for my liking.

She holds up her hand and I look at it for a moment before realizing she's expecting a high five.

"Result." She beams.

I feel a bit sick.

Anna pulls her coat on and we head down to the seafront. Because it's half term, the amusement park is open, and we're going to spend Mum's money on the thing I love best. (Besides Anna and Mabel and

Doctor Who and old John Hughes films and cake and chocolate and . . . well, it's one of the things I love best—let's leave it at that.)

It's sunny, but the wind is howling in our faces. The trees grow sideways, blown at an angle by the wind that never stops, even in summer. I sometimes wonder if everyone who lives here is bent at the same angle, and when we go away from the coast people notice us standing in office blocks and train platforms and wonder why we're at an angle, which I would know the number of, except I am appallingly bad at math.

As we walk, I tell Anna what happened with Gabe. The wind steals my secrets and whirls them up into the air, blowing them away.

I don't know why the flashing lights and the thumping music and the whirling chaos of the amusement park doesn't send me mad, but it does the opposite. After last night, it's like a sensory comfort blanket. We stop at the kiosk to change our money into tokens, then run to get to the waltzers, because we can see that the cars are filling up and we don't want to wait.

"I can't believe you haven't messaged him back," says Anna, squished up beside me. I'm holding on to the metal safety bar and she's swinging herself back and forth, trying to make the car move before we've even started.

"All right, girls?" A boy leans over the back of the car, and I reach up, handing him two tokens. It's cheap at this time of year, so we get twice as many rides.

He drops the money into his apron thing and grabs our car with both hands at the same time as the ride creaks into action.

"I don't know what to say," I reply, but the words are spun out into the air.

I laugh and laugh as we spin around and around, never fast enough, shouting for more when the boy twirls our car until there's a lull and Anna is gasping for breath and shoving her orange hair back out of her face before it starts again. We kaleidoscope in a spin of lights and distorted music and chaos. And I wonder why in the middle of all this, somehow, I feel safe, and ordered, and happy.

We stagger off afterward, with our legs all out of control, and lurch onto the wooden bench beside the cotton candy stand.

"D'you want some?"

"In a minute," I say, reaching into my pocket for the jelly beans. "We've got these, remember?"

"Where's your phone?" says Anna with her mouth full.

I pull it out of my pocket. I know that I need to reply to Gabe, but it's become a thing now, a big invisible solid thing, and I don't know how to climb over it or what to say. And I don't want today to be about that.

So I type **How about Wednesday?** and hit send with an unusually decisive tap.

Gabe, who clearly hasn't read the same rule book that I have (because aren't you supposed to wait and look cool before you text back?) replies straightaway.

Sounds good. Same place, same time?

See you then, I reply. And Anna, who has been looking over my shoulder and picking all the red jelly beans out of the bag while I did it, gives a little whistle.

"Impressive."

CHAPTER FOURTEEN

It's quarter past six and I'm rolling out of bed in the darkness to go to the stables when I realize the whirring noise I can hear is someone hoovering.

I don't do bleary half awake like Leah or Anna or Mum. I do asleep, which happens like a light switching off, or not for ages, so I lie awake with owl-wide eyes staring at the ceiling wondering why my brain won't stop whirling. But awake is unequivocal. It just snaps on, always early, usually before the rest of the world, and I don't like lying in bed because it makes me feel weird. Which is why having an early-morning sort of horse isn't the problem it might be for other people.

There's still no washing in the new world order that Eve has brought about, and as there's nobody to stop me I just pull on my dirty jodhpurs over yesterday's underwear because I'm going to have a shower later anyway and I'm sure Mabel won't care, because she wakes up every morning with green stains on her sides from lying in her own poo, so comparatively speaking I'm quite respectable, really. And I don't brush my hair because—well, I don't really like brushing my hair unless it's absolutely necessary, because it gives me the creeps and makes my shoulders go all prickly. So I shove it back in a ponytail and pull my black hoodie over my head and, no, I don't make the bed.

"Morning, honey," says Mum, in the hall, in her pajamas, shoving the hoover with one hand and holding a can of Pledge and a duster with the other.

I look at her with an expression which indicates that I suspect she's lost it completely.

"Ah yes," she says, bending down to unplug the hoover and standing up, itching her nose. She sneezes three times before continuing. "Just thought I'd get a head start, you know."

"Right," I say, still looking at her with my eyebrows in the air.

"Grandma?" she replies, and as she says it she leans over and scooshes a squirt of polish onto the wooden banister and rubs it, hard.

"If this is a guessing game, I'm going to need a bit of help here." I fish my boots out from under the dresser and sit down on the stairs to pull them on. I'm slightly concerned that if I don't hurry up she might start polishing me too.

"She's on the train. Gets here at two thirty."

"Did I know this?" I love Grandma. I don't love unexpected things that sneak up on me when I've got a day of decompression time planned with no people in it.

"It was *on* the calendar," she says, sounding a bit defensive.

I get the feeling Mum had forgotten too. Since Dad went on his shoot, she's been acting really weird.

CHAPTER FIFTEEN

"Hello, sausage."

I've only just gotten home from riding Mabel. When I open the door, the smell of hairspray and soft skin and dog fur and lovely things is in my arms and hugging me before I have a moment to object.

"I smell of horse," I say into Grandma's shoulder. She's wearing some kind of bobbly jacket thing, which is very pink and doesn't taste very nice when you get it in your mouth.

"Just as a Grace should smell," she says, and she sort of extends me out with her arms as if I'm an outfit she's trying to decide on. "Look at you."

"I can't."

"You funny bean," she replies, and gives me another hug. Leah skits past in the background and I can't help noticing she's got her hair in a neat ponytail and she's in jogging bottoms and a T-shirt, like she should be.

"Where's Mum?" The house already smells all Grandma-ish, and not just because she's arrived smelling of Estée Lauder perfume and old-person things, but because it honks of polish and I can see the sitting room floorboards are all shiny. Grandma gets up at half past five every morning and hoovers the stairs before she takes Elsa, her gigantic German shepherd, out for a walk in the park. So her house always smells of polish and floating dust and tidiness.

"I'm here," says Mum, and she appears in the hall, drying her hands on a tea towel, and she's wearing an actual apron. I'm slightly concerned that I've been transplanted by aliens into an alternate—but very similar—universe where things have gone back to the way they used to be, only sort of—shinier.

"How is that lovely pony of yours?" says Grandma, shooing me into the kitchen, where I sit down at the now-spotless table. I don't know where all the stuff has gone, but I can't help hoping that Eve's been chucked out along with it.

"Horse. She's a horse, because she's Arabian, and even if they're smaller than the official horse classification they're still horses . . ." I sort of trail off, because even I can tell when I'm doing the fascinating-facts-by-Grace thing sometimes.

Grandma doesn't say anything, because she's already rootling about in her handbag. "Here we are," she says, handing me a packet of mints. "I was buying a paper for the train and I remembered you said you were training her to take them from your mouth."

"Yes, well, we're not *really* encouraging that," says Mum, with her head in the oven. Not in a Sylvia Plath manner—not that I should be making jokes about that because it's very much not funny, obviously—but in a pulling-out-a—

"You've made *cake*?" I say loudly, and Mum gives me That Look, the one that I know means *shut up, Grace*. And I realize that while it's okay for me and Leah to bumble around all half term with no clean knickers while Mum drinks wine with Eve, apparently that's not okay for Grandma to know.

"She's always been a lovely cook, haven't you, Julia, my love?" Grandma beams across the breakfast bar at her.

"Thank you, Barbara," says Mum pointedly. "I'm in the can't-do-anything-right stage of parenting teenagers, as you can see."

I unwrap this month's edition of *National Geographic*, which has arrived in the mail, so I can sneak it upstairs to read in the bath.

ooo

Half an hour later, I'm still sitting at the table, utterly absorbed in an article about bear cubs. Mum's chopping vegetables by the kitchen sink, and Grandma's emptying the dishwasher.

"I'm sure you two can sort this out," I hear Grandma say over the clattering of mugs being replaced in the cupboard.

"Things aren't going to be the same." *Chop chop chop*, goes Mum. "I need to be bringing in money. Eve says—"

"Yes, but *Eve* doesn't have children, Julia . . ."

CHOP chop chop chop.

"I had noticed." There's a pause, and the sound of sizzling as something hits oil in a saucepan, and the room swirls with the smell of onions and garlic. "But my life can't revolve around being a parent," and I catch her half turn to see if I'm listening, so I turn the page of *National Geographic* and trace a finger across the top of a photograph of a wooden hut as if I'm utterly transfixed.

"Come on, Julia," says Grandma, leaning in really close to Mum's side, talking in a super-low voice. "You know Graham will always make sure you're okay—even if it does come to . . ." She trails off.

"While the girls are around, yes—but I need to secure *my* future as well."

I don't know why it is that none of them ever remember that I have bat-hearing superpowers. But I feel as if I'm hearing half a conversation and the rest is composed of Meaningful Looks.

I close the magazine and bang my hand down on the table in a decisive sort of way.

"Right, that's me off to have a bath now," I say, picking up the magazine and the packet of mints. I think Mabel won't mind if I eat them.

"Don't drop that magazine in the bath before your father has seen it, Grace, or it'll be me that gets the blame."

God, Mum's bad-tempered at the moment. I smile sweetly at her and disappear.

ooo

I'm running the bath and sitting on the bathroom floor playing a game on my phone when Grandma appears through the clouds of steam, brandishing a small blue envelope.

"I completely forgot. I met a very good-looking young man at the garden gate as I arrived."

I know Grandma's a bit desperate to make sure we're all married off, but trying to hook me up with the postman is a bit desperate. He's about forty—mind you, I realize, that probably *is* her idea of a young man. I take the envelope.

"There's no name on it."

"He said it was for you, dear."

I tear it open. Inside, there's a little metal TARDIS key ring. No note, no card, nothing else. I feel a fizz of nerves and excitement.

"No love letter?" Grandma sounds a bit disappointed.

I shake my head, and I can't stop the smile from curving upward, and I suspect that I'm going red, but hopefully she thinks that's just the steam.

"How odd. Well, I'm not surprised you've got admirers, Grace. You're clever and funny and I'm very proud of you. You need to open this window, darling," she says, reaching over the toilet and hooking it open so all the lovely clouds I've been creating puff out of the window and disappear. "Now, before you get in, I've got something for you in here."

She reaches into her bag again—it's always reminded me a bit of Hermione's beaded bag in Harry Potter. I get the feeling that if life got a bit much I could climb inside it and live quite happily on a diet of Werther's Originals and old-fashioned tins of travel sweets.

"I was hoping you'd all make it down to Kent as you have a two-week half term, but as you couldn't, I've brought these from Aunty Lou's bedroom. Seems a shame to have them sitting there gathering dust when you love them so much."

And she pulls out the three old-fashioned pony stories I love the best, and hands them to me. I run a finger across their crumpled age-spotted covers and sniff the edges of the pages, which smell deliciously of old things.

"Thank you." I sort of waggle them in gratitude, because I'm so happy that I half want to cry, but I don't want to cry, and I can't really get up and hug her because I'm on the floor and it seems too complicated.

"I knew you'd like them," Grandma says, and she turns and picks up the towel I've left on the floor, and she folds it up and puts it on the radiator. "It'll be nice and warm when you get out, that way."

ooo

We've eaten soup for tea, and Grandma's suggested that maybe she could help me tidy my room a little. When she said it, Mum made a snorting noise, which sounded like a dragon exploding, and Leah (who, predictably, likes to keep her room organized, because she would) burst out laughing.

"Are you serious? The last person who went in there was eaten alive."

"I've seen a lot worse than that in my day," says Grandma. "You should have seen your aunty Lou's room when she was a teenager."

Aunty Lou, who lives in a white farmhouse in Spain, is possibly my favorite person in the whole world. She breeds horses and has about ten wild cats with huge ears and long, enigmatic faces, which lie around like pet sphinxes all over the place. When I grow up, I'd like to be her.

"I didn't know that," says Mum. "Lou's place is always immaculate."

And it's true. It's all whitewashed walls and brightly colored woven rugs and space—so much space. It's quiet and cool and she lives there with Javier, her boyfriend, who is Spanish and kind. He gives us huge long strings of sweets when we go to visit. Lou spends so much time speaking Spanish that she forgets words in English sometimes.

"Oh, she was a horror," says Grandma. "So there's hope for you yet, sausage."

ooo

We've mucked out my room. It's not unlike clearing Mabel's stable except we didn't have a wheelbarrow. We might as well have, though. Somehow Grandma's persuaded me to get rid of a load of old clothes that were too small (which I've been holding on to for ages because, well, I don't like letting go of things), and there are nearly two black bags full of rubbish.

(I did say it wasn't exactly tidy in there.)

My phone pings with a notification and Grandma passes it over. "Anyone interesting?"

I can feel my face going pink, because when I look down at the message there's a gif of an exploding kitten in the TARDIS, which makes me laugh.

Grandma chuckles. "Is it a *young man*, Grace?" She puts down the bottle of cleaning spray that she's been using to clean the skirting board.

"He's called Gabe," I whisper. "Do NOT tell Mum." I put the phone back down on the chest of drawers, facedown, just because I already feel like I've said more than I meant to.

"Well," says Grandma, and she sits down on the edge of the bed, which has been stripped of all the covers and is waiting to be made up. She looks enormously pleased, and I don't think it's just because the bedroom now looks like it belongs in a magazine article. "That *is* interesting news. So is this Gabe the handsome young chap who delivered the envelope?"

I do a little sort of half shrug. "Yes."

"Well, my little Grace is growing up." She reaches across and gives me a squeeze on my knee.

I feel a bit sick again. Tomorrow is meeting-up-with-Gabe-again day, and I've managed to distract myself by working like a fiend at the stables, having a bath, and blitzing my bedroom. Now, with a gigantic surge of panic, I remember that I have to do the whole date thing all over again.

○○○

It's almost two in the morning and I still can't sleep. Everything is exhausted except my brain, which is just whizzing around and around and around. I've tried counting sheep. I've even tried listening to the relaxation app with the man with the annoying accent. All I can think about is tomorrow, and not screwing up by doing something weird or socially awkward.

What I need is a rule book.

I pick up my phone and search "old-fashioned etiquette."

CHAPTER SIXTEEN

ere's a short list of things I don't like.

    1. Surprises

    2. Bowling

"D'you want to just—"

Gabe sort of motions toward my feet, and my very much still-laced-up-thank-you-very-much Doc Marten boots.

There was nothing in Lillian Eichler's *Book of Etiquette* (published 1921, available free on Project Gutenberg, for those of you playing along at home) about the correct procedure for When Your Second Date Comes Around and He Announces He's Taking You to Lazer Zap and Bowl.

I know this, because I read the entire thing last night, and finally got to sleep sometime after five. This morning is the first I realized what people feel like when they can't get out of bed.

I had to literally drag my limbs from under the covers and I couldn't face cycling to the stables, so I caught the early bus there and back.

The heating on the way back caused the smell of horse to float gently out of my clothing and fill an area around me wide enough that office-dressed people were wrinkling their noses and looking unimpressed.

And then I had a shower. There was no Leah to help me get ready because she was at a tennis tournament with Mum, and Grandma had taken herself off to the garden center, which seems to magically lure in old people with the power of scones. So I just washed my hair and brushed it (ow) and left it to dry and, because there was nobody to tell me not to, I put on the same thing I'd worn to the party. There was a splodge of something on the front of the TARDIS, but I gave it a rub with a face wipe and it came off, mostly.

So that's how it started. I'm standing at the end of the road at lunchtime, waiting for Gabe, and he turns up in his plaid shirt again and a different T-shirt this time and he holds my hand, which is nice, and we start walking. A magpie hops onto the wall in front of us and looks at me beadily. Because I once read a book on superstitions and accidentally absorbed a whole load of them, I have to salute him surreptitiously and mutter, "Morning, Mr. Magpie. How's your wife?" under my breath. If Gabe notices, he doesn't say anything.

"I got us tickets for bowling," he says brightly.

Everything in my entire body shrieks, *EMERGENCY, EVACUATE SITUATION.*

I carry on walking, and make what I hope is a polite sort of noise. It sounds a bit like "MmMMPH."

"You been up to much?" says Gabe as we walk along the road that leads down to the shore, where the big shops and the very loud bowling place live. It's funny that even though he's grown up here he's still got a soft Polish accent. It must come from listening to his family. I wonder if he speaks Polish at home, or if they only talk English.

"Just riding Mabel," I reply, adding uselessly, "my horse."

Gabe looks at me sideways and gives a grin that makes his eyes scrunch up and he looks incredibly cute as he says, "I know who she is."

"Can you ride?" I realize that on a conversational scale this isn't exactly up there, but my brain is not being helpful. In fact, I think it might be realizing that it needed more than an hour's sleep. Your fault, brain, I think. I could have done with you on my side today.

"Yeah, a bit. My cousin Petra has horses back in Poland, and when we go over in the summer I help her look after them."

"You could have a ride on Mabel sometime," I hear my mouth saying.

I don't let anyone ride Mabel, so I have no idea what is going on with the whole brain-to-mouth connection, but I can tell that this isn't going the way that I'd hoped.

I don't know how to bring it up, so I sort of lift up my left hand so he can see that I've got the metal of the TARDIS key ring circling my thumb, and the blue box tucked inside my palm.

"Thanks."

There's one of those five-minutes-long seconds when he doesn't say anything, and I think maybe I got it wrong, and there's a random "very handsome, darling" young chap turning up on the doorstep handing *Doctor Who* merchandise to unsuspecting grandmothers.

And then Gabe smiles. "I thought you'd like it."

So we trundle toward our inevitable doom (or the bowling alley, if you want to be technical) making weird, stilted conversation about nothing. I'm not sure why it's so awkward, or even if it is. But I'm so tired I'd quite like to lie down and have a sleep on one of the seafront shelters where the old people sit and watch the world go by.

It doesn't get better when we get inside, because it wasn't ever going to, really. The thing is, what I ought to have said was, *Sorry, look, I'm really tired, and autism and crashing music and flashing lights and bowling noises and arcade machines are a really bad combination.* It's weird because it works at the funfair—I think because there's loads of fresh air and the noise gets carried away by the wind. But here we're trapped inside the darkness and it feels like everything is taking over my head. Instead of saying what I feel, though, I smile politely and allow myself to be led by the hand into sensory hell.

So here we are now, and I'm looking at a shelf full of shoes that other people have put their feet in, and I'm wondering who decided this was a good way to spend time.

"I'll get you some shoes," Gabe says, "if you tell me what size you need."

I think that's what he says, anyway. I can't hear very well and now my brain's doing that thing it does where it sort of goes on a

delay

so

when

someone

speaks

I

watch their mouth move, but the processor takes a moment to translate the words and by the time I've caught what they mean they've started to say something else. It's like watching a film where the words are out of time.

This was not in the bloody etiquette guide. And now I'm wearing someone else's shoes, and frankly, wearing someone else's shoes is not my idea of a hot date.

So we set up the bowling lane with our names in the machine and I feel hot dread because I am beyond awful at bowling and I say to Gabe in his ear, which smells nice and of apple shampoo this time:

"I'm awful at this."

And he turns around and puts his mouth close to my ear, which makes the backs of my knees feel prickly, and he says, "Everyone says that. I bet you're not."

After about half an hour it's clear to everyone—Gabe, me, the group of ten-year-old boys having a party in the next lane—that I really am. And not comedy bad, just pointlessly, humiliatingly, no-spatial-awarenessly bad.

It stops being funny and starts making me feel like I want to burst into tears. And the music's so loud that we can't really talk about anything.

So we go and get a coffee and some fries to share in the cafe bit, and Gabe checks his phone and fiddles with the plastic knives and forks and makes a stack of salt packets. He seems distracted and sort of strange, like he's somewhere else. I can't think of anything to say at all, and neither can he, and I wish more than anything that I could make it all be like it was the last time when we had a nice time and there wasn't all this noise and elephants crashing in my head.

"Shall we forget the next game and just get out of here?" says Gabe.

I hear that bit loud and clear, and I nod, but I feel a bit sick because this isn't the way it was meant to go. I was going to ask nice questions about his family and how they came here from Poland and what he thought of school and if he thought the Doctor was going to regenerate in the next series. And instead we're leaving the bowling alley, and the skinny boy with the matching Lazer Zap and Bowl baseball cap and polo shirt asks if we're not playing our second game and Gabe says, "Nah, mate, thanks."

As we leave, Gabe reaches for my hand and he pushes his other hand through his hair and gives me a smile, and I think, actually, maybe, this isn't as bad as I thought. Because now we're outside, and we start—without either of us saying anything—walking along the little promenade toward the park.

My hair's whipping around because of the wind, and I stop for a moment to shove it behind my ears.

"It looks bonkers, doesn't it?" I say, because I know that I'll have a mad halo of fuzz all around my head. Living by the seaside and having hairbrush issues is a really bad combination.

"No." Gabe shakes his head. "It's nice."

And he sort of half turns toward me and reaches out a hand, pushing back the same strand of hair I've just tried to tame. But he doesn't put his hand back. It strays down the back of my neck and somehow his mouth is on mine, and—in the street, *the actual street*—he kisses me. And I don't know how it happens, but I reach out and put my arm up so it curves around the side of his waist and I can feel his breathing and underneath his shirt and his T-shirt the heat of his skin. And I kiss him right back.

I pull away again for a second because it's too much, and my heart is thumping so hard that I swear everyone in the street can hear it. I—me—Grace—I'm kissing a boy in the street.

He grins and he looks a bit breathless too. "Shall we go to get an ice cream?"

I feel myself smiling back at him. "Yes."

We start walking toward the park when he looks down at his phone again. It's bleeped in his pocket about five times.

"Look, I'm really sorry—I need to nip into my house for a moment. D'you mind if we just—?" He stops, biting his lower lip and frowning.

I shake my head. "No, it's fine."

"I'm really sorry."

Gabe's house isn't far. When we get there, his mum opens the door. Her hair is dyed a cool burgundy red color, and she's got the same brown eyes as him. She smiles at me and steps back, beckoning us into the hall. There are coats hanging neatly on a rail, and a long row of shoes paired up underneath the radiator. It smells of the fabric conditioner on Gabe's clothes, and furniture polish, and a vanilla-scented candle, which is flickering on the window in the sunlight. There's a huge black-and-white aerial photograph of fields and a farm hanging up on the wall.

"Grace, it's very nice to meet you."

She knows my name. That's a bit weird.

"Hi."

"You like the picture?" Gabe's mum looks at me looking. "It's where I grew up. My sister Jana still lives there."

"Oh, the place with the horses?" I look at Gabe, but he's disappeared through the doorway into the kitchen. He's facing the sink, and as he turns, nodding, he places a glass tumbler upside down on the draining board.

"Yes, we visit in the summertime." His mum pushes her hair back from her face, tucking it behind her ear. She looks at Gabe. "You okay?"

Gabe rubs down his hands on his jeans, leaving wet smudges. "Yep."

"Good boy."

"I'm not a dog." He grins at her and turns to me. "Ready?"

I've been waiting there the whole time, so, yes, of course I am. I nod, though.

"Bye, *kochanie*." She ruffles his hair and he ducks out from under her hand, laughing.

"Lovely to meet you, Grace," Gabe's mum repeats as he pulls the door shut, almost as she's still talking.

"Mothers." He shakes his head and looks a bit embarrassed.

"What does that mean—*kochanie*?"

"Um, I suppose—sweetie, or darling? That sort of thing."

It's funny when you see people from school who seem like these huge, fully formed characters by themselves and suddenly they're at home with a house that smells like baking and their slippers are in the hall and you realize they've got messy bedrooms and have to help with chores too.

"Sorry about that," says Gabe, breaking into my rambling thought circle. "I had to—" He pauses for a moment before all the words come out in a tumble. "I've got these pills I have to take twice a day 'cause I've got ADHD. I forgot to take them with me."

"What happens if you don't?"

"Best case—I end up a bit spaced out and I'm crap at paying attention. Worst—well, that's why I ended up moving schools."

For some reason we both stop and sit down on one of the benches that look across at the big wooden climbing frame in the gardens by the lake. It's new, and it's so busy that from here it looks as if it's been invaded by a swarm of ants. There are children running around the sides, up the climbing wall, along the tunnel. There's one banging a huge stick down on the roof of the lookout shelter, and I realize that the parents below are yelling at him to get down.

"There you go. That's the sort of thing I used to do. Only sort of louder and bigger and messier. And pretty much every day. Like someone had forgotten to turn on my dangerous-stuff filter." Gabe points to the kid on the climbing frame. As we watch, the father starts shinning up the pole on the side. The mother is on the ground looking up, her eyes shaded from the sun with a hand. She looks terrified.

"I spent a lot of school sitting outside the principal's office." Gabe shifts sideways so he's facing me more. He picks up the string of his hoodie and pulls out the threads, untangling them, his mouth twisting sideways in thought. "When they finally worked out I had ADHD and I wasn't actually as much trouble as they'd thought, Mum and Dad decided it would be better if I moved schools and started all over again."

"Because you had a reputation for being tricky?"

Gabe laughs. "Tricky. I like that." He reaches out a hand and I watch as our fingers touch, one by one, like starfish. We hold them there as I speak.

"Me too."

I'm surprised I say it. It sort of falls out of my mouth. Gabe raises an eyebrow in question.

"Except autism, not ADHD. I was the weird kid in primary school." I pull a face and I feel my face prickle with heat but I don't stop talking. "I mean, weirder."

"I *like* weird," says Gabe, and he pushes his fingers against mine a tiny bit, like a little pulse. It feels nice.

"Lucky. Anyway, now that I'm older I don't take backpacks full of fossils on school trips to London, or lie on the floor in H&M hooting. Or have meltdowns in the classroom." I think about the moment when they handed me the time-out card so I could escape before the feelings began to boil over inside me. "Well, not much, anyway."

And for some reason this makes us both giggle and we start laughing at the idea of it and then Gabe does a sort of honking noise.

"Like that?"

I do a sort of whoop.

"More like that, I think."

"Hoooot," says Gabe.

"HOOOOT," I say back, and an old man passes by and shakes his head at us.

I do a little small-owl sort of hoot.

"*Hoot?*" says Gabe thoughtfully, but he's still laughing.

"That's a socially acceptable hoot, Gabe, well done. Good hooting." I pat him on the knee and he grabs my other hand in his and leans forward and says, "Hoot," in my ear and I feel his breath on my cheek and I turn and I kiss him, because I can.

And then we get up and start walking again.

"So, apart from the hooting situation," Gabe says, swinging my hand, "what's it actually like?"

And I think for a moment, because people don't actually ask that very often. They tell me what they *think* I feel because they've read it in books, or they say incredible things like *autistic people have no sense of humor or imagination or empathy* when I'm standing right there beside them (and one day I'm going to point out that *that* is more than a little bit rude, not to mention Not Even True) or they—even worse—talk to me like I'm about five and can't understand.

"It's like living with all your senses turned up to full volume all the time," I say. And I stop and he sort of spins around so he is looking at me. "And it's like living life in a different language, so you can't ever quite relax because even when you think you're fluent it's still using a different part of your brain so by the end of the day you're exhausted."

And I think about getting home from school and the effort of making it through the noise and the lights and the people and the change and the cars and the smells and the sun and the rain and holding it together through all that, and then getting home. And how when I get home and I can switch off, that's when I blow up, because it's safe.

"Wow," says Gabe.

I nod. "Yeah."

And then I say that we should go to get some ice cream.

ooo

"Do you want strawberry sauce on that, love?"

The man at the kiosk on the prom has served me ice cream a million times. I've said no thank you (I don't like stuff on stuff) a million times. But this time I say yes, because right now, this second, my life feels like someone's covered *me* in strawberry sauce and chocolate sprinkles *and* hundreds and thousands. And I look across toward the shore where the lights of the amusement park are sparkling even in the daylight and I feel all sparkly too.

"All right, mate?"

It's Gabe's best friend, Archie. I'm standing with a dripping ice cream and Gabe turns around, licking his, and gives a bob of his head. "Arch. You going down the skate park?"

Arch does some kind of complicated thing with his scooter in reply. It goes from under his feet into the air and then back under his feet again in seconds. "Yep."

He pulls at the strap of the helmet he's wearing, so his shaggy blond hair flops down over one eye, and he gives me a nod too. "All right, Grace?"

I say hello in a formal sort of way, because I'm not very good at impromptu informal conversations that I haven't been expecting. I realize that if I don't do something rapidly, the rivulet of melting white ice cream and oozing red sauce is going to start pouring over my fingers and that is going to make me feel sick. And I preferred sparkly and breathless to that.

"I've just worked out how to do a backflip," says Archie. "Want to come down and look?"

"You mean scrape up the pieces and call an ambulance when it all goes horribly wrong?" Gabe slides a sideways look at me.

"He's funny, isn't he, Grace?" Archie shakes his head, laughing. "You're funny, Gabe. Very droll."

"What d'you think, Grace?"

"That would be lovely," I say politely, because frankly this afternoon can't get much odder. It's like an out-of-control dodgem. I keep veering from one feeling to the next. Maybe this is what dates are like. I don't have anything to compare it with, so I don't know.

"Go on, then," says Gabe. "We'll catch you up."

"Cool," says Archie, and he wrinkles his nose when he smiles, and I think he's pleased we're coming.

And our hands sort of find each other again, and we walk down toward the pier and along the marine lake path. Old people sit on benches watching the ducks and swans floating by, and families are laughing their heads off as they try to control the little wooden rowing boats.

We walk up the path and into the skate park and I have to force myself to keep walking because there's a whole clump of people—I can't pick them out to start with, because my contact lenses don't work as well as my glasses do, and I'm hopeless at recognizing people. Because of this I've developed a fairly standard sort of polite (I think, but remember I am the Queen of Resting Bitch Face) half smile, which I keep in attendance while I work out who I'm smiling at.

I have this weird thing, where people outside their normal spaces confuse me. When I see people from school that I don't spend time with, it takes me a moment to work out who they are. When they're in uniforms and in the corridors and they're hanging around with the same people they always do, I can recognize them almost straightaway. Put them in everyday clothes, mix them up so the populars are hanging around with the geeky science lot, and the skater boys are talking to the netball team people, and I am confused. Beyond confused.

"Gabe, hi!"

It's Holly Carmichael.

Of course it is. And on the bench, poking around inside a huge shopping bag from H&M, there's Riley and Lauren. And whatever her name is, the other one with the dyed black hair that looms in the background chewing gum and looking threatening, is looming in the background looking threatening. Apparently it's her full-time job, even in the holidays.

Holly bunches her hair over to one side, letting it fall loosely over one shoulder.

Gabe waves a greeting at her, then gives my hand a squeeze and turns to me, lowering his head so his mouth is near my ear again as he says, "We'll just watch Arch doing his thing then head off, shall we?"

As I nod a reply, which he feels rather than hears, I see Holly looking directly at me, her chin raised slightly as if she's sizing me up. And I see her look down at Gabe's hand in mine.

"So, what are you two up to?" she says as Gabe turns away from my ear so we are facing them, side by side, holding hands, like cutout dolls. "Not wearing your *Doctor Who* costume today?"

I wish I could send her into deep space. "No."

"Did you *know* Grace was a total geek?" Holly says innocently, smiling at Gabe as if she's being perfectly lovely. She somehow manages to radiate charm in his direction while simultaneously beaming hatred in mine. It's an interesting talent. I realize I'm probably glaring at her, because my face isn't very good at disguising what I'm thinking.

"Yes," says Gabe, and he sort of swings my hand. "We've been comparing notes on our favorite episodes."

"Really?" says Holly, and both her eyebrows shoot up for a moment before settling back down like two fat slugs. "I had no idea *Doctor Who* was so *fascinating*." And I think that she's unsettled all of a sudden, and that's not a thing I've seen before. I watch her rearranging her face.

"Yeah," says Gabe, and he smiles at me as if we're sharing a secret.

"Right." Holly flicks her hair over her shoulder and plucks at the strap of her vest top that's showing underneath the checked shirt she's wearing, so we can all see what brown shoulders she's got, and it's as if I literally don't exist. "Maybe you can explain it all to me."

She gives me a frosty glare. I realize that Holly Carmichael is now looking at me as if I've got something she wants, and she's not very happy that I've got it. And I'm standing here in the skate park holding its hand. *His* hand.

"Look," I say, and I point up at the ramp where Archie is doing some kind of complicated spinning thing with his scooter. He looks down at me and his smile is watermelon huge and he leaps into the air and lands on the edge of the ramp before flying down and up into the air and over, so he flips 360 degrees and lands—safely—on the ramp. It makes me feel a bit sick.

I give him a thumbs-up and a big smile to indicate how impressed I am. Holly looks at me with utter disdain and shakes her head, so I feel myself blushing.

I realize that I've made myself look like a presenter from kids' TV, and I slink my hand down to my side.

It's all going a bit weird, and I feel really awkward about talking to Gabe about being autistic, like I've exposed part of myself, and I feel sort of raw. I really, really would quite like to just go. But I'm not sure how to say that, so after another five minutes, when Gabe turns around and says, "Shall we go?" I almost gallop toward the exit.

And I don't know whether Gabe doesn't have anything to say or if he's just bored, or whether it's just me feeling weird. It occurs to me much later that maybe he's shy too.

"So, your mum seems nice," I say, realizing I sound about a hundred years old. "What about the rest of your family?"

We stand waiting at the crossing.

"What d'you mean?" Gabe looks a bit puzzled.

"How did you end up here?"

And instantly as he's talking I'm thinking—is it okay to ask that? Is that rude? Is he thinking I'm rude? So I'm listening to his reply, but the voice in my head is asking questions at the same time, and it makes it really hard to concentrate and I start thinking maybe I'm acting strangely and my ears start doing that thing they do when they whoosh in time with the ground as I'm walking. I just want to lie down and have a rest.

"Oh," says Gabe. "Well, my mum and dad moved here when I was only tiny. And then my grandmother came over when my grandpa died, and my uncle Piotr got a job one summer and ended up staying, but my aunty and uncle and cousins still live on the farm in Poland."

"It must be very difficult living with all your family in one house squashed together," I say, because I can't imagine having that many people all taking up space and there not being anywhere for quiet and to hide and switch my brain off.

"No, it's fine," says Gabe.

"Oh," I say, and we walk along the road in silence. But it doesn't feel like a companionable Anna sort of silence, and the whole time I'm searching through my head for things to say, but all I can think of is that I wish we could go back to the nice bit before all the awkward bits. And I wonder if dates are supposed to be like a roller coaster of amazing bits and uncomfortable silences and kissing and not knowing what to say.

We end up at the corner of my street, and Gabe lets go of my hand.

"Right, then," he says. And he leans forward, still with a look on his face that I can't quite read, and I'm not sure if he's trying to kiss me on the cheek to be polite or on the mouth because he wants to, and so I duck my head sideways at precisely the wrong moment and I think he gets a mouthful of hair.

"Holly Carmichael likes you, you know."

I didn't mean to say it.

And Gabe looks at me with a frown of surprise and says, "Really?"

I say, "Yes, it's obvious, because if you've studied body language you can tell because she turns herself to face you and she was mirroring your gestures and she flicked her hair, which is a grooming motion that is used to—"

And I stop halfway through the sentence because, honestly, I need a minder sometimes to hit me over the head with an inflatable mallet when my mouth starts going and my brain forgets to catch up.

"Right," says Gabe. He steps backward. "I better get back."

"Me too," I say.

He looks at me for a moment with a strange expression on his face, just before he turns away and walks down the road toward town.

I watch and watch until Gabe becomes a little speck, and then he disappears from sight.

And I don't know how, but I think I've blown it.

CHAPTER SEVENTEEN

And that's that, because this is real life and not a film, so I turn around and start walking toward home in the just-starting spots of rain, running my hand along the bumpy bricks of the garden walls as I go. The sky is grumbling gray and it feels as if any moment now it'll start tipping it down, but I like the smell in the air. I love sitting inside watching the rain, but I don't mind getting soaked either, so I don't rush. I'm too tired to rush. Being *on* for a whole afternoon is exhausting, and I can feel my legs dragging as I walk.

I sort of want to text Gabe and say, *Look, it's not just that it feels like the volume of all my senses has been turned up. But things are* complicated, *and it's not that I don't like you, it's just that getting through the day is tiring, and I'm sorry my brain flatlined.* And I wonder what it's like having ADHD and I sort of want to ask about that too. But I wouldn't even know where to start. The thing is, I don't know how to say to someone new, *Um, you know, if I act weird it's not me acting weird.* And it's awkward trying to figure out how to tell people or what to say. Sometimes I wish I just wore a Ten Facts About Being Autistic badge, which could answer all the questions, and I could just point to it.

Then, of course, he might just reply, *Yeah, the thing is, I'm just not that into you anyway, weird or not*, so actually maybe I'll just switch off my phone again and not think about it.

CHAPTER EIGHTEEN

After my bath, all I want is the kitchen to myself, and Withnail sleeping on a pile of washing on the table. Sometimes I think I'd like to retire from being a person and just quietly live under the kitchen table with a book and a packet of cookies.

What I get is—not that.

"Honestly, Barbara . . ." Mum's back from the tennis tournament. She's folding up a tea towel that's already folded. She's shaking it out and straightening it proprietorially, so it's just the way she likes it. "I wasn't planning on making anything much for dinner this evening. The girls don't need to . . ."

"It's fine." Grandma takes the tea towel out of her hand, and smooths it out slightly before sliding it into the drawer beside the oven. I can see Mum's nostrils flaring, which is what happens when she's pissed off and trying to hide it. They're having land wars over kitchen equipment. "You have your night out with Eve," and Grandma sneaks me a look as she says it, just a tiny one, sideways, "and we'll have a nice girly evening, won't we, Grace?"

Mum turns around. "I didn't hear you come in."

My stealth mode is highly effective, but no match for Grandma radar.

"She's been here five minutes, Julia."

"Where have you been, then?" Mum rubs her head in confusion, so her hair fuzzes up around the crown and sticks in the air.

"Just out," I say, and I stack up a pile of papers that are strewn in front of me on the dining table, more to distract myself than because I've suddenly become super organized.

"Careful with those, darling," says Mum. I look down at the papers. They're old, curled-up notes with DURHAM UNIVERSITY FACULTY OF EDUCATION stamped across the top of them.

She comes over and gathers them to her chest protectively. "They're notes from my teaching degree. I was just looking something up for that job I was telling you about."

Grandma makes a disapproving sort of snorting sound as she chops onions. There's a hiss as she slides them into a saucepan, and she turns back to the kitchen island to wipe the surface before sprinkling it with flour and rolling out a huge blob of pastry. I swear Mum rolls her eyes at this.

I like it when the kitchen is all fuggy with cooking and smells like home. Since Dad left this time, the place hasn't been right, and Grandma coming has fixed everything. The only person who seems unimpressed with it all is Mum, and that's only because Eve's too-cool-for-everything attitude seems to have rubbed off on her.

I look down at my phone in case there's a message from Gabe, who must be home by now, but it's blank. The last message I sent Anna isn't showing as delivered, so she's probably had her phone confiscated or something. I watch as Mum and Grandma take part in a sort of territorial kitchen war. Mum is now putting away the dishes that Grandma has just washed.

"They're not quite dry," says Grandma. "Let me get you a tea towel—just a moment."

"It's fine," says Mum, and I can hear her teeth are gritted. She's always had a sort of Grandma threshold when she comes to visit, where she goes past being delighted at having someone else to help and tips over into there's-an-extra-person-in-this-house mode. Not that she'd ever admit it, of course, but I watch it happening from my quiet corner.

"I can't think how you're planning to make this job work with Graham away as much as he is," says Grandma quietly.

"Other women work."

"Of course they do, Julia, but other women don't have . . ." There's a sort of pause, the kind of pause you get used to if you're me. "Well, they don't have the same *things to consider* as you do."

"It's not the same as when she was little, Barbara."

"No, but you're forgetting Leah. And you've leaned more on her than you should have, just because she's sensible. She's still only thirteen."

Mum flicks a glance across the room at me to make sure I'm not listening, but I'm hidden beneath my hair, picking at a bit of loose nail, apparently oblivious. I'm feeling slightly sick at the thought that the whole Gabe thing has ended in the usual Grace disaster, but I'm trying to be Zen. All right, I'm failing to be Zen, but there's not much I can do.

"Grace is about to turn sixteen. She's growing up."

I sit very still because I don't want a birthday conversation to start. It's there on the calendar, looming. And I don't like birthdays. Without thinking I start tapping my finger and thumb together—*taptaptaptaptaptap*—to try to stop my brain from shooting off into a panic. I'm not doing my birthday until Dad gets back. We've arranged it already. I start preparing the speech in my head just in case they've forgotten, but—

"And it's time I put my money where my mouth is. What kind of role model am I?"

There's a puffing noise from Grandma, and I can imagine her face, even though her back is toward me and she's stirring the chicken stuff for the pie.

"Role model?"

"The girls have grown up thinking I'm here to be at their beck and call. I don't have a life outside this house."

I cock my head sideways slightly at that, before I realize that any movement might end the whispering and they'll remember I'm party to the conversation.

"You've been doing volunteer work at the center for six years."

"Yes," Mum says, but it's a sort of exasperated hiss, "volunteer work. Eve says—"

"Eve." Grandma manages to make that one name into a whole sentence, and a question, all at the same time.

"It's substitute teaching," says Mum carefully. "That's all."

"And I think it's a lovely idea in principle, but these girls need you." There's a second where Mum opens her mouth to protest. "Leah needs you."

"Leah's fine," says Mum, shaking her head. "She doesn't need hand-holding. She's responsible, and she's always been the capable one." Mum's voice is low.

I scowl at this. It's true, but it still makes me feel a bit crappy. When we were little, I remember Mum would send us into soft play with Leah holding my hand, acting as protector when I didn't want to deal with galloping hordes of other kids throwing unexpected things at me in the ball pit. And when we went swimming, even at nine she'd be the one who remembered to fasten the locker key token around her wrist and remember where we'd left our stuff. I was unpredictable, prone to wandering off in a dream if I was thinking about something interesting, likely to forget where I'd put things. Leah didn't have meltdowns when everything got too much and the world felt all scratchy.

"That doesn't mean you can just opt out because your friend Eve has come along and put ideas in your head."

"This has *nothing* to do with Eve," says Mum. "I'll have bills to pay and two children to keep. I've got responsibilities. We can't all go swanning off to the other side of the planet whenever we feel like it."

She's talking in that pointy way she does when she's about to shout. Except she won't shout at Grandma, because she never does.

"I think the two of you should be sitting down and having a look at your priorities. In my day, you didn't just bail out the moment things got tough."

There's a clang as Mum shoves the saucepan full of vegetables onto the burner and spins around. And then there's a dangerous-feeling silence, which lasts for a long second.

"I'd love to," says Mum, "but, in case you've missed it, he's not bloody here."

She lifts her pile of papers as I look up, realizing that I can't pretend I'm not there anymore, and she looks me in the eye for a moment. There's an expression on her face I haven't seen before, and it makes me feel weird in my stomach.

"Right, then. I'm going to get ready. I'll leave you two to get on with your baking."

And she stalks out of the room.

CHAPTER NINETEEN

am sixteen.

Charlotte had the whole school in a barn for her birthday. I creep up to mine with my finger on my lips.

Mabel and I have been out in the sparkling morning with nothing but birds to keep us company, and we're both sweating from too much cantering. I pull the saddle off and sling it across her stable door before I pull my phone out of the back pocket of my jodhpurs. I would've read the message when I was riding, but Mabel was dancing on tiptoes the whole way, skittering sideways with every whisper in the grass.

It's Anna. I read with Mabel's nose hooked over my arm, sniffing in the hope of mints or something nice in my pocket. Her breath steams up the screen.

HB, my lovely chum. Starbucks, 11am.

She knows that even the words make me feel weird and self-conscious and prickly. This is why we're friends. She gets it.

Ok. Might be five mins late. Need to de-horseify.

I slide into the seat opposite Anna. She's got our favorite table upstairs, looking over the pedestrianized shopping street, where we can gaze out of the window and make up silly stories about random people. When you sit downstairs, you end up feeling like you have to leave when your drink's finished, but up here the staff seem to forget you're there. We spend hours sometimes, watching the world go by.

Anna's got a blob of chocolaty cream on the end of her nose. She's already ordered me a drink—a bucket of hot chocolate with a precarious mountain of cream on top—and two huge slices of our favorite chocolate cake.

She slides a package across the table. It's a shiny gold paper envelope, and when I open it a sprinkle of purple glittery stuff scatters across the table. Inside there's a tiny, perfect silver unicorn on a chain.

"Thank you." I feel a bit awkward, and motion to my nose then hers. She wipes the blob of cream off and licks her finger thoughtfully.

"You're welcome, un–birthday girl."

"So. Moving on from the fact that you are now legally entitled to join the armed forces, work as a street trader, and get married—with parental consent—"

I look at her and waggle my eyebrows.

"—as well as *lots* of other things," she continues. "First of all, you didn't reply to my *what happened on your date with Gabe?* question. So I want all the details."

I put my hand down to my pocket automatically, remembering her message. When I got it last night, I was standing with Mum and Polly, looking at Mabel all tucked up for the night in bed, and I'd put it away in my things-to-think-about-later brain file. Then I'd got home, it was Grandma's last night, and we'd ended up watching Dad's television program all together. And by then I was completely overpeopled, and I'd gone upstairs to comfort-watch three episodes of *Walking with Dinosaurs* and fallen asleep with the light on.

"I was walking Nan's dog at the park yesterday afternoon," Anna continues, hugging her drink with both hands. She's sort of peeping over the top at me. "I bumped into Archie."

"Literally?" I remembered him clattering through the park on his scooter, flying down the stairs in one leap with a clash of rubber wheels and metal on tarmac. Bumping into Archie was potentially painful.

"Not literally. As in, *Hi, how are you?*"

"Oh, right."

"Right," says Anna, and I realize that there's a tiny catlike smile curving up over the edges of the mug.

"Right?"

"Right." She does a sort of comedy eye roll.

"Okay." Well, here we are. None the wiser, but with two cups of hot chocolate to our name.

Anna looks at me with an eye-popping face, and waves her hands up and down. And I realize what she's saying.

"*You* and *Archie?*"

"Er, no." Anna giggles. "No *me and Archie*. But he asked if we were going to the park today. Apparently, there are loads of people from school going down, and Jamie is bringing a drone thing to do a video for his YouTube channel. He asked if I—if we—if we were coming."

I feel a sort of lurch of panic. I couldn't work out if I was supposed to text Gabe or not, so I haven't. And he'll be there, and I don't know what I'm supposed to do about that. I'd like to see him. However I do *not* want a whole mortifying everyone-remembers-it's-Grace's-birthday-and-stares-at-her thing.

"Oh, good," I say cheerfully.

"Grace, that is the crappiest impression of someone being pleased about something I have ever seen."

"Oh." I try to rearrange my face a bit.

"Now you look like you're about to start growling." Anna giggles.

I try again, arranging my features into what I hope is "excited and enthusiastic" coupled with a jolly sort of thumbs-up.

Anna shakes her head, still laughing, and puts down her mug. "D'you know what? It's better if you just don't try."

"I'm having trouble accessing the appropriate expressions from my memory vault. Please excuse me." I pull a face.

I manage to keep her talking about pretty much everything apart from how yesterday went. Not because I don't want to tell her, but it's just—Gabe hasn't messaged me, I don't know what to say to him, and I feel awkward. Even by my day-to-day stratospheric standards of awkward. And the truth is that there's so much *stuff* going through my brain all the time that it's just another thing to worry about, and I don't need that right now.

"I love you and your silly face," says Anna. "Anyway, I like him. He makes me laugh. Will you come with me? Pleeeease?"

"To the park?"

Oh, joy.

"Sure." Anna's almost bouncing on the spot, and I'm not going to wreck it for her by being That Friend. Even if I'm having a minor internal meltdown. I take a gulp of hot chocolate and look out of the window.

"Do you think this looks okay? Do you think I should go back and change?"

Anna, as always, looks perfect. Her orange hair is plaited over one shoulder, and wild curly bits have broken loose and are twirling prettily around her neck. She's wearing a fluffy gray cardigan and black jeans with a purple T-shirt and her new purple Doc Martens that she got for her birthday. I'm in yesterday's hoodie, which is—if I'm honest—slightly Mabel-smelling, and jeans, and my ancient comfort Vans with a hole in the toe.

"No changing. You look amazing."

Honestly, life would be far easier if someone handed out a *How to*

Be a Human Being handbook with subsections for stuff like "What to Do the Day after a Date in Which You Told Your Boyfriend Your Nemesis Likes Him." Except, of course, it would also have to have a sub-subsection called "How to Know When the Person You Kissed Stops Being a Person You Kissed and Becomes a Boyfriend." Except if it was a girl you kissed, obviously. You see what I mean? Life is a complicated thing.

"What are you thinking about?" says Anna, and I realize I've been staring out of the window with a glazed expression again.

"Uh. Nothing." I love her, but I think I might make her head explode if I explain all that. "When d'you want to head to the park?"

"Dunno. Now?"

ooo

There's nobody at the park apart from a gang of mothers with small humans in strollers and slightly bigger humans tottering along beside them. All the small ones have snot emitting from their noses.

I know about the small people's noses because they end up flocking around me and Anna when—trying to act like we are just casually hanging out at the park and not waiting for some mythical everyone'll-be-there episode, which hasn't transpired—we buy a couple of paper bags of duck food from the little cafe, and sit on a bench throwing handfuls onto the ground, so the entire bird population of the northwest has come to hang out with us.

"Well, we're popular in the bird universe." Anna looks at me sideways as she holds out a palmful of corn. The bravest duck waddles up and starts eating from her hand.

"Me have some?" says a small bobble-hatted being. She steps forward, leaving her two little friends hanging back. We give the little people some corn and they throw it, hopelessly uncoordinated, into the sky. It rains down on the ducks.

"Here," says Anna, tipping the bag so that the food falls into their little starfish hands. "Have some more."

125

We watch the small people bumbling about for ages. We're surrounded by ducks and darting moorhens, and small, toddling, miniature humans.

"Phoebe, are you terrorizing those big girls?"

One of the stroller mums comes over, smiling apologetically at us. "Sorry, she's mad about ducks."

"She's in the right place." I gesture to the eleven million that are orbiting our feet.

"Yeah, we are veritable duck magnets," says Anna.

"With no friends," I add under my breath.

"With NO friends," Anna echoes.

The woman gives us a slightly odd look and shoos her small offspring out of the duck collective, back toward the swings, where the other stroller mums are gathered, drinking coffee and handing out bags of chips.

"So here we are. We have three new toddler chums and a flock of ducks who want to be our new BFFs, and the park is empty of all the amazingly cool and interesting people who were supposedly going to be hanging out here today." Anna shakes out the last of the duck food and folds the paper bag into smaller and smaller squares until it is minuscule.

"Maybe they're coming later?"

Anna looks a bit deflated. I'm used to the whole being-in-the-wrong-place-at-the-wrong-time thing. It's sort of what I do. Anna—despite being my friend, and therefore having a sort of perpetual uncoolness download attached—still has the hope and optimism of youth. It's my job to cheer her up.

"Let's go for a walk around the park and down to get fries. By the time we get back, maybe Archie and everyone will have arrived to do amazing, spontaneous holiday things, Disney-movie-style."

"Are you trying to cheer me up?" Anna says darkly.

"Did it show?" I say. "Was I good?"

"Uh, no," says Anna. "But fries are always good."

"Two small chips and a bottle of Diet Coke, please."

"D'you want salt and vinegar on that, love?"

"Nah, I'm all right, thanks," says a voice. I turn around to see Archie grinning at my shoulder, his scooter under his arm. His helmet is a bit wonky, and I can't help thinking that it isn't going to keep him safe if he falls over. Then I remember that I probably don't need to give him a helmet-related health-and-safety lecture, so I don't say anything.

"You made your mind up about that vinegar, love? Your chips are getting cold."

"Oh. God. Sorry." I turn the other way where Anna is standing, eyes wide, not saying a word. She sort of nods mutely.

"Yes, please," I reply.

"You coming up to the park?" Archie motions outside, where I can see Jacob, Jamie, and Tom on bikes.

"Yeah," I say, "we were just heading up there."

Anna gives me a little sneaky look and we make our way out of the chip shop.

Tom is hopping on his BMX in an irritating manner. To be truthful, it probably wouldn't be annoying if I weren't having a *where is Gabe?* panic and scrutinizing the horizon like a maniac.

"Where's Gabe?" asks Anna, trying to sound casual. I can feel my face going absolutely scarlet from my forehead right down to my neck, which is not a good look.

Archie pushes back a lock of his hair that has fallen down over his eyes, shoving it back under the side of his helmet so he can see when he turns to Anna. He must like her, because Archie basically spends his whole life under his fringe, so if he's making the effort to actually look her in the eye, well . . .

"Oh, he's got some family thing on today. I called for him on the way. Said he might bike over later if he can escape."

We wheel, scoot, and walk our way through the park.

As if it were some prearranged thing, everyone stops at the circle of benches in front of the duck pond. Archie flips his scooter in the air and lands it back on the pavement with a metallic thud. A couple of unsuspecting ducks wheel into the air, quacking their disapproval.

"So, you two been up to much today?" Archie asks.

"Nope," says Anna, sounding casual. "Nothing much. Just thought we'd wander over, see what was going on."

"Mummy! The big girls!"

Phoebe, the small red-coated bobble person, beetles toward us, waving her hands.

"More duck food?"

Archie turns to Anna, a questioning expression on his face.

"You girls must know all these ducks by name by now," says the mother of the small person as she scoops her child in the air, her legs flying upward.

At the same moment, the entire duck collective spots Anna and me and—hopeful of another epic picnic—they all hurtle toward us and flock around our feet.

"Is there something going on here I'm missing?" asks Archie, looking at a mallard pecking at the lace of Anna's Doc Martens.

"No." Anna lifts up her foot, and the duck steps back, looking angry. (Turns out ducks can look angry. Who knew?) "No, we're just duck magnets, apparently."

"Never seen them before in our lives," I add helpfully. Anna starts giggling.

"Right," says Archie, shaking his head but smiling. "You two are weird." He does a hop-spin thing on his scooter, during which time I look at Anna and we both pull the same face. So much for looking like we're just, y'know, passing by. Now we look like weirdo duck-obsessive park lurkers.

"I saw your sister earlier," says Tom. He's turned his BMX upside down now, and is swearing at the chain wheel, trying to get the chain to sort itself out. "She's down at the kiosk with Lily and Emma."

"D'you need a hand?" As the wheel spins to a stop, the chain still slightly off, I lean forward. I pull at the chain where the teeth are caught and manage to untangle the part he was having problems with.

Tom looks at me, impressed. I'm not sure why he looks impressed, because presumably we all learned to ride bikes at the same time, meaning we all also learned how to untangle bike chains. I straighten up and wipe my hands on my jeans.

"Thanks." He flashes me a grin, and it takes me right back to primary school and wobbling our way through bike-safety lessons with luminous yellow jackets on. "I forgot you were really good at bike stuff."

"'S all right." I push my hair out of my eyes and realize I've probably just covered my head in grease smudges.

Something weird happened when we all got to about thirteen. We went all the way through school hanging out together in a big amorphous gang, having known each other since nursery school in most cases. But as soon as we got to high school, everything got weirdly awkward and everyone settled into boy-girl groups. I always liked being friends with the boys. You know where you are with them. But the girls were different. Holly and her lot were caught up in complicated politics before I even knew what was happening, back in second grade. I remember being told I wasn't allowed to play a game because I didn't have the right color pink T-shirt, and crying all the way home from school. Mum, clearly trying to do the right thing (I think even then she was wondering why I stood out like a small, cross sore thumb), bought me an identical T-shirt to Holly's, but I refused to wear it. Being seven was complicated.

Being sixteen is apparently even more complicated. Now we're in the park, and Archie's doing some kind of bizarre scooter-related mating ritual, trying to impress Anna with his ability to hop on and off metal benches. The small people and their parents have finally left, and the ducks, sulking at the lack of extra food, have made their way back across to the little island in the middle of the pond and are sunning themselves.

I'm not quite sure what to do with my arms and legs. Or my face, for that matter. It's not until Anna's attention is elsewhere (and it is—because she's laughing and making the appropriate noises of entertainment and approval at Archie's scooter techniques) that I realize how much I rely on her in situations like this. Left on my own, I run out of everything.

But it's okay, because just when I thought things couldn't get any more awkward, I see a shape in the distance and recognize the walk. My stomach sort of jerks with nerves, and my knees feel weird. When I'm already dealing with people and noise and ducks and small children, it's a bit alarming.

"All right, Gabe man," shouts Archie, throwing one arm up in the air in greeting. Anna spins around to look at me, her eyes wide. She's got pink cheeks and her hair is wild around her face, and she looks lovely but a bit different—like she's not quite *my* Anna, and I feel a wave of something not-quite-nice passing over me.

I have no information on this. The nonexistent rule book for dealing with social situations would be really handy here. Do I kiss him on the cheek to say hello, like you'd do with a relative you haven't seen for a while? Am I supposed to sidle up to him in the manner of a television sitcom girlfriend and smile adoringly at him? (Never going to happen—don't worry. I've not had a personality transplant.)

And who is he with? I don't recognize this person. I am quietly flapping my hands against the sides of my thighs in minor panic mode. Inside I'm having major panic mode. I could just run off and say that I saw a duck drowning or something.

"How you doing, man?" Jacob and Tom stretch out to give Gabe high fives as he reaches us. I look at my shoes because I don't know what else to do. Anna says hi to him, and when I look up (which I do sort of while still keeping my eyes on the floor—don't ask, it's compli-cated) I can see she's giving me That Look. The look that says, *Grace, you're not humaning properly.*

I look up at Gabe, who ducks his head and grins.

"Hi," I say, but it takes a tremendous physical effort to get the word out, and I look back down at the ground again.

"Hey." Gabe gives me his crooked-front-teeth smile again, and pushes up the sleeves of his shirt.

And my mouth blurts out (I don't know why; there's no connec-tion between my brain and the things it does), "Is Holly coming?"

Gabe's eyes drift down toward the ground for a second, and I al-most think he looks a bit embarrassed. And then he looks up at me and says—

"I don't know." And his tone is almost a bit—I don't know, it's sort of *brave*, or something. "I've no idea. We only came down because Arch texted me and said you were here."

My toes feel like they're going to explode, and there's a sort of weird whoosh that goes from my hair to my feet and back again and I just stand there for a second because I can't quite believe Gabe just said that out loud.

"This is Marek, my cousin." Gabe seems to be telling everyone this bit. "He's over from Warsaw for the week—his mum's working at the university." I look up again, and Gabe is looking proudly at his cousin, still with his arm draped over his shoulder. Marek gives me a small, shy sort of smile, and I feel a bit better because he's not the only one who feels awkward.

"Marek, this is Jake and Tom"—they both nod in greeting—"and you know Archie."

Archie nods and says, "All right?"

"I'm Anna," says Anna, smiling openly in that lovely, straightfor-ward way she has. I have no idea how she manages to make being a person look so uncomplicated.

"And this is Grace." Gabe smiles directly at me, and for a second he catches my eye and it feels like it did when we were just on our own.

"Hi," says Marek, and we all sort of stand there for a bit.

Sometimes I think it's not just uniforms that school's good for. It sort of makes sense of the social stuff too. When you've only got a fifteen-minute break between lessons, and lunch is from twelve thirty until one fifteen, and you've got to fit lining up in the cafeteria and going to the bathroom in there too, there's not enough time for things to get awkward. You sort of squish your interactions into little tiny chunks, and the classroom stuff is monitored by teachers (even if they're hideous) and everything is ordered and easy to deal with. Put us in a situation like this, where we have the whole afternoon to hang out at the park and do nothing, and we're at a complete loss. We need someone to organize us with a game of rounders or some sort of wholesome activity. Otherwise we'll spend the entire day wheeling around these benches making uncomfortable conversation about nothing and waiting for something to happen. That's why the bikes are useful. At least when you've run out of things to say, you've got a sort of prop handy, and something to do with your hands.

"Gabe tells me you are big fan of *Doctor Who*?"

Marek balances on the edge of the bench beside me. His accent is lovely. He talks quietly, fiddling with a key ring he's got in his hands. Unthinkingly, I reach for the TARDIS key ring, which is now hanging from the zip on my purse. He sees it and reaches out.

"Can I see it?"

"Sure."

"Cool," says Marek. "I would like one of these very much."

Gabe looks across, seeing us talking. He's chatting to Archie, but his face looks pleased to see that I am talking to Marek.

I grab desperately around in the air for something to talk about and land on Gallifrey. Not literally, unfortunately. That would be nice.

"D'you think we'll see River Song in the next season?"

Marek visibly relaxes, sitting back against the bench, folding his hands behind his head. It's funny when I can see other people feeling what I'm feeling. I guess being dragged out to meet a load of strangers isn't that pleasant for him either.

"Well, the nights on Darillium are twenty-four years long, so I think that perhaps we will."

"I hope so."

I love River. I'd quite like to be her when I grow up.

I'm about to carry on talking when someone puts their hands over my eyes.

"Guess who?"

Anna's in front of me, talking with Archie and Gabe. The boys have set off for the skate park on their bikes.

"No idea."

The voice sounds familiar, but the vague getting-it-wrong panic makes my ears not work properly.

"Guess!" says the voice again, urgently. I squirm sideways to try to get out from the hands, and they let go as I turn around.

"Could you really not get it from my voice?"

It's Leah, who (a) wouldn't normally do something like that because she knows it would freak me out and (b) doesn't sound like herself because there's a bit of an edge to her voice that isn't normally there because she's with Holly's sister Lily and that gang again.

"Where's Meg?" I ask automatically. I'm so used to Leah and Meg being inseparable in the holidays that it's weird to see her hanging around with other people—especially when the other people are so hideous. I have no idea what Leah's up to. Holly's sister is a smaller, even pointier-faced, just as mean-looking version of her sister.

"Not a clue. Why d'you keep asking me that?" Leah says cheerfully. "What you up to?"

"Dunno," I say, looking at Marek, who checks the time on his watch.

"I have to be back home by four," he says, shading his eyes from the sun as he peers across at Gabe. "Mama said she's taking us out for pizza."

I look at my phone to check the time. I don't want to be late for Mabel this afternoon. I'm rubbish at getting out of situations. Sometimes I end up staying places for hours longer than I want to because I don't know how to make my excuses and leave. I'm about to shove my phone back in my pocket when a text from Mum (festooned as always with poo emojis, because she discovered them about six months ago and thinks they're the most entertaining thing ever) appears.

Darling are you around? I've left the key on the table and locked myself out.

Leah checks her phone at the same moment, then turns the screen around to show me. Same message.

"I'll go," I say, at exactly the same time that she says exactly the same thing.

Standing around for another hour feeling awkward while Anna admires Archie's scooting technique isn't really at the top of my things-to-do list. And Gabe being here is weird. It's almost too much, this feeling of wanting to be near him. I keep looking to see where he is and catching his eye and realizing he's looking at me. But we keep talking to other people instead, like we're sort of skirting around each other.

Leah shakes her head. "I need to get back anyway. I've got training later." She hops onto the low wall, arms out to the side, pointing her toes.

I check with Anna in case—and I think it's unlikely—she wants to head back across town now. But she's wrapped up in Archie and it's nice to see her smiley and having fun, and, frankly, she'd probably be better off without me there being awkward, so when she says, "D'you want me to just come back now?" with a sort of reluctant expression, I shake my head and tell her I'll message her later when I get back from the stables.

"Are you two heading back now?" Gabe says, and looks across at Marek.

"Yeah," says Leah casually—and I feel jealous that she doesn't stumble over her words and get tongue-tied when she chats to Gabe. "Mum's locked herself out."

Marek raises an eyebrow in question at Gabe. "We need to be leaving soon, I think."

"Walk us along to the roundabout, then?" Leah jumps off the wall, and shoves her phone back in her jeans pocket.

I'm almost sure she does it deliberately, but she hangs back, telling Marek to wait with her while she tells the girls she's leaving, so Gabe and I end up walking along the path in front of them. And we walk along together for a bit before it almost feels too weird to be walking with our hands side by side without reaching out for his, because I can feel the heat from his arm radiating through to mine, so I stretch out a finger, tentatively, and another, and then—I hold his hand. And he gives me a sideways look and a smile and sort of swings my hand a bit in his, and we walk up to the roundabout with Leah and Marek tagging behind us.

ooo

"You were *holding hands*," says Leah with a little squeak. "It's like *actual* loooove."

"It's like actual nothing very much yet, thank you very much, and if you say anything to Mum I will literally kill you with my bare hands." I give her the Look of Death so she knows I'm serious.

Leah zips her mouth shut with her finger, her eyes wide open.

She notices the TARDIS key ring and takes it out of my hand. "Nice."

"It's from Gabe," I say, and I feel a bit proud.

"You need to get him something, Grace," says Leah, and it seems so obvious now that I can't think why I didn't think of it. That's what people do. They buy nice things for each other.

"Anyway," says Leah after a moment, "my lips are sealed."

"Yeah," I point out, "they better be. If she finds out you've been down to the amusements when it's completely banned, you'll be in the shit."

"Point taken." Leah nods, grinning.

It feels like it's been ages since I've spent any time alone with her. We walk along the familiar road together, our feet on autopilot, past our old primary school. Inside the classroom, Mrs. Bedgrove, our second-grade teacher, is sticking bright-colored letters to the window, even though it's the holidays. She catches a glimpse of us and waves, smiling.

"Why's she working?" Leah frowns, looking at me.

"That's what teachers do."

"In the *holidays*?" Leah looks horrified.

"Yeah. I read about it in one of those educational-supplement things Mum keeps leaving all over the kitchen table. They work all the holidays and in the evenings and they never get time off."

"Right," says Leah. "Why's Mum wanting to go back to that, then?"

"Dunno."

"Grandma's not impressed."

"It's fine," I say, teasing. "Apparently, I'm old enough to know what I'm doing now and you're *the responsible one*, so we don't have to worry about what you're up to."

"Right." Leah pulls a face that I can't interpret. "As long as Mum thinks that, we're sorted."

I don't really know what she means by that. I know that Mum's still under the impression that Leah and Meg are best friends, and I suspect that if she had any idea her beloved youngest was hanging around with Holly's sister and her gang, she'd be seriously unimpressed. Or would she? Now that Grandma's gone back to Kent, we'll be back to living in chaos and Eve hanging out of the back door, leaving Marlboro butts all over the step. I shudder at the thought.

We walk for a while longer, past the dentist where Leah bit the hygienist's finger when she was five.

I run my hand along the bumpy wall and the smell of warm stones in the sunshine reminds me of being little again and holding Mum's hand, stumping along in red shiny wellies, jumping in puddles while Leah sat in her pushchair. I think of bobble-hatted Phoebe, our little duck-feeding friend. I miss life being that simple. Life was much easier when there was a hand to hold and you knew where everything was.

"You having a nice nonbirthday?"

"Yes, thanks."

Leah pulls a face. "I think you're just hoping if you postpone it until Dad gets back you'll get extra presents."

Leah gets the birthday thing. It has to be the same every year: pizza, in the same restaurant, at the same table, with a silly hat and helium balloons, which we take home. It's what I like. My idea of hell on earth would be a surprise birthday party. Every year I feel relieved when I get it out of the way and nothing hideous has happened.

"Leah?"

It's easier to talk when we're walking side by side. I haven't had a chance to speak to her in ages.

"Mmm."

"D'you mind Mum going for this job?"

Leah and I used to talk much more before this last few months happened and everything started shifting under our feet. She was always in my room sitting on the bed, or I'd be in hers. She didn't count as people, so she didn't wear me out. She was just sort of part of the furniture, but since Dad went away this time, everything seemed to change. Or maybe it's because Eve has appeared and our little triangle of family has been broken.

"Dunno." She cracks her chewing gum in a way that would give Grandma a fit. "Everything's gone a bit—weird. I don't like Eve. I keep hoping it'll go back to normal once she's gone."

"Me neither. It's like she's stolen Mum and given her a brain transplant."

"Zombie brain eater."

"Personality stealer."

"She's worse than Holly Carmich—" I begin, and stop myself almost as the words come out of my mouth. I don't suppose Leah wants to hear me slagging off her new best friend's big sister.

"That's basically what Grandma said," Leah says, and I don't know whether she's heard what I said and is agreeing, or is carrying on from before. "She told me yesterday morning that everything would go back to normal when Dad got home and Eve finished her contract and went back to London."

"Hmm."

"Yeah."

It doesn't feel like that to me.

CHAPTER TWENTY

"Ahh, look at that, both babies to my rescue!" calls Mum over the garden wall, her shape blurry through the hedge.

I've got the keys in my hand, and as I turn into the drive I'm waving them aloft, but my arm freezes in midair when I realize that Mum's not alone. I turn to Leah, talking through clenched teeth.

"Why is *she* here?"

"No idea," says Leah. She juts her jaw slightly, and looks across the front garden at Eve.

"We just popped out to have an afternoon glass of wine to celebrate," Mum begins.

"Of course," says Leah to me under her breath.

Mum's smile disappears, and I can see Eve sizing us up as if she's won something somehow, as if she thinks she's got more right to Mum than we do.

"I had some good news today from the substitute teaching agency," Mum continues, her voice slightly strained. She's in let's-all-be-happy mode.

I paste a polite smile on my face. The truth is if I didn't think Eve was behind all this—and I didn't think it was because she was on some sort of mission to make Mum forget that we actually exist—I'd probably be pleased she was going back to work and getting out of our way, except I don't really like things changing and, well, anyway. I'd be a *bit* pleased. Even if—with Dad AWOL half the time on his globe-trotting expeditions—it would effectively leave us a bit lacking in the actual parent department.

Mum takes the keys from my hand and unlocks the front door. I give Eve a wide berth and skirt around her, scooping up a traitorous Withnail, who was about to prowl through her legs in the hope of food.

"Grace, honey. Let's go out for something to eat to celebrate."

I stop dead, standing on the porch as if my feet have been glued to the floor.

"We'll pop by the stables on the way—you can sort Mabel out quickly and we'll wait in the car."

"What?"

"It's not every day your firstborn turns sixteen," Mum continues, her voice breezy and tight. She's not leaving any space for me to object. "I know you don't want to do anything for your birthday, but Eve thought we should all go out as we've got two things to celebrate . . ."

"Happy birthday, Grace," says Eve. I don't look at her, or reply.

"I don't want to go." I really, really don't want to. What on earth is she doing? (A) I don't do last-minute changes of plan and (b) I don't deviate from my birthday routine. No, no, no. No thank you.

Leah pauses in the doorway with her finger on her lips, looking thoughtful. She clearly doesn't want to go either—let's face it, who *would* want to spend a night out with cow-face?

"I've got training," she says, pulling her tennis shoes out from under the dresser.

I beam her a silent wave of gratitude.

"You can miss one session," says Mum, pulling out her phone from her bag. "I'll text Hazel and tell her you're going out for your sister's birthday. It's not like you're in the habit of skipping training."

"They won't have enough people for doubles."

"Leah," says Mum, with the exact tone she usually uses on me, "I'm sure they'll be fine."

Leah puts the shoes down on top of the dresser, in a move designed to piss off Mum, who is weirdly superstitious about shoes on tables. Mum picks them up and holds them in her hand as she turns to me.

"We can have the same table as always," she says, trying to appease me. "And we can do your meal when your father gets back too."

"I don't want to."

"I'm not having any arguments. Eve's been good enough to help me get an interview for this job, and we are bloody well going out to celebrate." She fixes me with a look.

"I was going to ride Mabel."

"You rode her this morning."

"I was going to ride her again."

"Grace." The Look again. "We'll pop by the stables on the way, sort Mabel out." She glances at Eve. "You don't mind waiting, do you?"

Eve shakes her head.

What's amazing is that through all this Eve is just standing there in the hall, not saying anything, just watching us. Not even pretending to avert her eyes and secretly eavesdrop (Eves-drop—ha), but she's just standing there with that smug catlike smirk on her face and her too-tight skinny jeans and her super-shiny expensive handbag over one arm.

"Why should I?"

I let Withnail down, reach into the dresser, and pull out my yard boots. Then I sit down on the carpet where I am and start pulling them on. I'll just take the bus up now. There's nothing she can do to stop me.

"Because your mother's worked hard for this, and you're being rude and ungrateful," says Eve in her clear, low voice.

I shoot a look up at Leah, who is standing above me. It's hard to argue your point coherently when you're sitting on the carpet and all you can see is everyone else's knees.

Leah flares her nostrils in a way that looks exactly like Mum and I swear she does the smallest shake of her head. *No,* I think it says, *don't make a fuss about this.*

I haul myself up in my yard boots and stand, facing Eve, in the hall.

"Fine," I say, but I glare at Eve with my absolute best death stare. She looks back at me like she's a cobra or something else equally venomous and generally horrible and unfriendly. You'd think seeing as she's friends with Mum she might make at least some effort not to hate me and Leah, but—apparently not.

"Right, well, as we're only going to Preselli's, we don't need to get dressed up." Mum checks in her handbag, pulls out a hairbrush, and runs it through her hair in front of the hall mirror. Eve smiles at her and offers her a red lipstick.

"You don't have to actually start dressing like twins, you know," I mutter, half to myself. "You've already got the same tops, the same shoes, and now you're in the same lipstick. It's freaky."

Leah kicks me in the ankle and I yelp.

"You ready, then, Ju?" It's not a question—it's a command. Eve turns to open the front door.

ooo

"Who's that waiting in the car?" says Polly as we clatter around from the field, Mabel trotting beside me.

"Mum's new—well, old—friend. Evil Eve." I'm quite impressed with that nickname. Don't know why I didn't think of it before. "She's up here doing some work project, and has basically moved her entire life into ours."

"Why evil?" Polly screws up her eyes to focus on the faraway car, a hand over her forehead to block out the last of the evening sunlight.

"She hates me and Leah. She seems to think we're surplus to requirements."

"Right."

"And she's basically forcing Mum to go back to teaching."

Polly looks at me sideways. "Forcing? What is she, a slave trader?"

"No, but she's done the whole *your life is a waste, all you've got to show for it is your offspring, you're a failed human being* thing."

"Hmm." Polly turns back to the hay net she is stuffing. "I can't imagine your mum being forced into anything she didn't want to do."

"And," I say, pushing Mabel's food bucket into the stable and closing the door, "where do we fit?"

"Where do you *fit?*" Polly starts laughing. "You don't need your mum to be holding your hand all the time. And Leah's more than capable of looking out for herself. Your mum needs a life—I'd go mad if I were her, stuck at home all the time when your dad's off doing the glamorous-explorer bit."

I slide the lock across Mabel's door and turn around to look at Polly, who is tightening up the drawstring on the hay net.

"I'm not saying I want her *stuck at home all the time*," I say, feeling a prickle of guilt. "I'm just—I don't like things changing all the time."

"That's what things do," says Polly reasonably.

"Well, I don't like it," I say, and walk back to the steamed-up car.

I climb in the back beside Leah and we head toward the restaurant.

ooo

"Table for four?"

The girl at the door looks harassed, her hair escaping in fine wisps from her ponytail. She's got a splodge of something red—sauce or wine—on the front of her white apron, and her cheeks are flushed pink.

"Yes, please," says Mum.

"This one okay for you?"

She shows us to the little booth at the back where we always sit.

I slide into my usual space, and for a second I think maybe this will be okay. There's a family of six sitting opposite, their smallest child banging something loudly on the plastic table of his high chair, and a little person who is five or so weeping snottily into a bowl of macaroni.

"Actually," says Eve, picking up her bag and leaning over to the waitress, "we'll have that table by the window, thanks."

Mum opens her mouth to say, no, it's fine, we're okay here—but Eve shoots her a look, and the frazzled-looking girl flushes a bit more and says, yes, of course, and leads us across the restaurant to the huge table—which should sit eight—in the window.

"We don't want to be cramped in that grotty little booth," says Eve, settling back against her chair, stretching her long legs out so they take up half the space under the table. She looks over the menu at Mum.

"This is nice, actually, isn't it, girls?" Mum says brightly, looking at me, then at Leah, who has her phone out and is scrolling through messages. "Leah, off the phone, please."

"Not really," I say loudly.

"Grace." A raised eyebrow. Mum looks up at the waitress. "Two glasses of the Shiraz and two Cokes, please."

"I don't think taking up a table meant for eight people when there's only four of us is very nice manners," I say, looking sideways at Eve.

"We're paying for a meal," she responds, her tone crisp. "We're not at a kindergarten. I don't expect to be surrounded by children."

"Should've left us at home, then," says Leah, surprising everyone.

"Leah!" Mum sits back in her chair. Leah doesn't do smart comments, or being rude, or rebellious anything. She does quiet, reasonable, calm, well behaved. I do rude and sarcastic.

"But it's your birthday, Grace," says Eve, taking a glass of wine from the waitress.

I shoot a silent look of horror at Mum.

"Your birthday?" says the waitress. "How lovely!"

She perks up at this and swooshes my napkin onto my lap, lean-

ing over me in the process so I can smell her shampoo. I sit rigid, trying to deal with the personal-space invasion.

Eve smiles at Mum. "Can you believe it?" She turns to the waitress. "Julia doesn't look old enough to have a sixteen-year-old, does
she?"

"Shut up, you," says Mum, going pink and looking pleased with
herself.

"Well," says Eve, raising her glass in Mum's direction, "you've done
your time."

She takes a swig of wine and clinks her glass. "To your new job
and your new future. And to freedom."

"Freedom," says Mum, and a funny look crosses her face. And then
she turns to me and says, "And to my beautiful girl, of course. Happy
birthday, darling."

I scowl at her and don't reply.

"You girls. I can't believe you're not even pleased about your mum's
job."

Eve looks at me and Leah and tuts crossly.

"I'm sure they are pleased—in their own way," says Mum, taking
another mouthful of wine.

My phone buzzes in my pocket and I slip it out and look at it under
the table.

I hate her, says Leah.

Me too, I type back.

"If you ask me, Graham's been allowed to spend far too long
thinking the world revolves around him," Eve says to Mum, who
pins her with her stop-talking look and somehow sort of nods at the
same time.

"Shall we get olives and dipping bread to start, girls?" says Mum
brightly. Not waiting for an answer, she motions over the waitress and
asks for them to be brought as a starter.

Eve swallows half her wine in a gulp.

"You need to have a life of your own, Julia. These two are old enough to fend for themselves, aren't you?"

She looks at me and Leah, and I want to kick her in the shins.

"To be honest, I don't see any reason why you couldn't go full-time. My mum wasn't running around after me when I was your age."

"Leah's only thirteen," I point out, turning to Mum. "And you've always been around and I think it's all very well for *her* to come marching in and start telling you that you should disappear off and work full-time and leave us to do everything and go to school, but—"

"Grace," she says, putting a hand over mine, "nobody's saying I'm going to be working full-time."

"Nobody's saying you can't, though," says Eve, actually clicking her fingers for the waitress. I didn't think people did that in real life. "You don't really expect your mum to be sitting around the house waiting on you hand and foot, do you?"

Ignore her, she's a bitch.

"Ciabatta and olives?" says the waitress, leaning between Mum and Eve, just at the right moment.

Megabitch, I reply, typing it into my phone while smiling sweetly at Eve's big moon face.

I take great pleasure in eating all the nice olives and leaving Eve the horrible ones with big lumps of garlic in the middle so she'll stink like a pig in her business meetings tomorrow. Leah eats all the bread and "accidentally" sticks her finger in the oil and vinegar more than once when she realizes that it makes Eve shudder with disgust. I feel a bit guilty that we're spoiling Mum's celebration meal, but if she hadn't taken Bitch Face out we could have had a perfectly nice time. In fact, if Bitch Face weren't in the equation at all, we'd be having the same perfectly nice time that we have every other time Dad goes away. It's not our fault that Eve-il has decided to land herself like a cuckoo in the middle of our nest. I glare at her again.

And then just when I think it can't get any worse, it all goes horrendously wrong. I go to the bathroom and when I get back there's a tangle of silvery helium balloons floating above our table. I pull out my seat and sit down, feeling sick.

"Who did the . . ." I begin.

"Eve had a word." Mum gives me a look that is somehow pleading and parental at the same time. *Don't make a fuss*, it says. I swallow and sit there, stiff with horror, and listen as the noise of the restaurant and the metallic whisper of the balloons and the slurping and the crunching and the swallowing fill my head and the room is a swirling kaleidoscope of sensations and noises and—

"Yes, that's lovely, thank you."

As the back of the chair behind me crashes into mine, I turn reflexively.

"Oh, sorry," says a voice, and I realize it's Holly Carmichael at exactly the same moment she realizes I'm me and she fixes me with her icy blue eyes.

"Oh, sweet," she says, so quietly that only I can hear. "Baby's first birthday party. Try not to wet yourself this time." She gives me the once-over, looking me up and down. I realize I'm in yard boots and there are wood shavings stuck to the bottom of them. I watch her indicating my shoes to her cronies with an arch of her ridiculously fake eyebrows.

"Nice boots."

I ignore her and pull my chair in tighter toward the table, hoping the lights overhead mean that my scarlet face doesn't show. But the already terrible meal is now completely ruined, and I'm hanging on by my fingernails. Now I feel like I'm too big for my chair and the food's getting stuck in lumps in my throat. I curl my fingers underneath the seat of the chair, holding on tightly and rocking slightly, counting to ten in my head over and over.

The waitress clears our plates and the room dims unexpectedly. I turn to Leah, and she shakes her head almost imperceptibly.

"Don't," she says, as the lights begin to flicker on and off in time to some tinny-sounding music coming through the speakers.

And I realize I've seen this before when I've been here and other people have been celebrating birthdays. And I realize that Eve is looking at me expectantly and Mum is looking at me with a pleading expression and the music suddenly unjumbles in my head and I realize what I'm hearing is "Happy Birthday Sweet Sixteen" and I want the ground to open up and swallow me whole. If I could actually just dematerialize in this moment, I would be quite happy. And I know, without turning around, that a sparkler-covered ice cream sundae is coming my way. And I know that Holly Carmichael will never let me forget this.

This is beyond anything that I have ever experienced, horror wise. I've turned to stone. Leah picks up the sundae and eats some, saying that I always get too full for dessert when we come here. I'm not sure I can even move.

Mum calls the waitress over and pays the bill while Eve readjusts her perfect lipstick in the bathroom.

"Oh, hello, girls!" Mum stands up, turns, and smiles at Holly. "Out for a meal?"

"Yes, thanks, Mrs. Armstrong," says Holly with a sickeningly sweet smile. "It's Lauren's birthday, so we're just having a little celebration. Ours is a bit more low-key than Grace's, though."

She flashes a look at me, and I want to die on the spot.

"Have fun," says Mum, who used to help out at nursery school, and remembers Holly as an angelic little round-faced five-year-old. Holly gives me the sickly sweet death smirk when Mum's back is turned, and there's a muffled sniggering as we walk out.

"I can't believe you did that." I glare at Mum as the door shuts behind us and I realize why I hate Eve so much. She's just a grown-up version of Holly.

"Oh, Grace," says Mum, ruffling my hair in what she thinks is an affectionate manner. It feels like she's raking my head with knives and I pull away. "Holly's harmless. You need to stop being so sensitive about girls like that. Grow a bit of a thicker skin."

She hooks her arm through my elbow and gives me a sort of jollying-along nudge. I leave my arm hanging straight down in the hope she'll get the hint. I don't feel particularly jolly.

I am sixteen years old. I hate birthdays. I have just been publicly humiliated in front of the absolute worst person possible and I am never, ever going to live this down.

And I realize I'm tired of this. I'm sick of being awkward and feeling like I don't fit and everything's uncomfortable. We're driving back home and my face is pressed against the cold of the glass and the smell of the rubber strip along the edge of the window and it feels safe—well, safer. I can retreat. And then I realize the answer is glaringly obvious. All I need to do is find something that means everyone will think of me as someone who is interesting and funny and nice, and not the weirdo that stands out all the time.

I look out at the darkness of the beach, and I have the perfect idea for how to make it happen.

CHAPTER TWENTY-ONE

My phone vibrates against my cheek.

You up?

It's Anna.

Of course I am. I'm still playing over the delights of my birthday celebration.

Very much so.

You amazing being of wonderfulness. I love you. (Imagine an Anna-style festival of emojis here.)

Right. I type in the darkness. **Are you OK? Just it's**—I squint more closely at the screen. Without my contact lenses in, everything's fuzzy around the edges.

—it's half past midnight.

I know I know I know. Can't sleep. Archie walked me back from the park. Eeeeee.

I smile at the thought of Anna's excited face. Right now she's probably bouncing up and down in the bed we broke, and if she's not careful it's going to give way again.

Did anything . . . happen?

NO

. . .

(There's a pause where I can see the little dots on the screen that indicate she's typing something, then it disappears. Then it comes back again. And then it disappears.)

ANNA, you are doing that thing . . .

. . .

Spill. You can't say no then use the disappearing dots of doom to leave me hanging here in the middle of the night. I'm a morning person—you're a night person. I am ASLEEP.

. . .

Oh, Grace, he's so . . .

. . .

CUTE.

Five minutes of waiting and I get "cute"?

(It's not like Anna to be lost for words. This is serious.)

Like *cuter than Howl* cute.

That *is* serious. On the official Grace and Anna Cuteness Register, Howl (of *Moving Castle* fame) is the pinnacle of gorgeousness. Yes, I know he's an anime character, but that's a minor detail. Go and watch it and come back and tell me you're not in love with Howl and then we'll talk. And then we'll make you watch it again until you are. I might just give up trying to sleep and watch it, actually.

OK, that is major. What're you doing tomorrow?

Hideous school shoe shopping hell with Mum in the morning. Want to meet me at the shore in the afternoon? I told Archie I might be there at two-ish.

I look at the screen for a moment and think about another afternoon of hanging around while the boys wheel around in circles and Anna chats to Archie and I don't know what to say to Gabe.

Let's meet there and have a beach party.

I type the words, thinking about my decision last night. I have to make some changes. I need to work out how to be one of them. I need to start fitting in. I want to be cool.

Here? You do realize we don't live in Venice Beach, right?

Yes, duh. You've got those portable barbecue things in the garage left over from summer.

We do?

It never ceases to amaze me how unobservant people can be. I was in Anna's garage the other day and saw them stacked up on top of the chest freezer.

Trust me, you do. Stick one in your bag. I'll bring matches and marshmallows and steal some sausages and stuff from the fridge. You do the same.

I can see it now. Late afternoon on the beach, everyone sitting around a fire, making s'mores, chatting and laughing. We'll be just like something from a film. And absolutely no Holly.

Mum's not even going to notice there's stuff gone from the fridge. She's on another planet most of the time. I can steal her secret chocolate and cookies for s'mores. Oh, this is going to be *so perfect*.

OK? I type.

OK, Anna replies.

OK, I return.

This is all getting very John Green, Anna types. **You mean OK as in see you there?**

Yes, that one. Let me know what time.

You're a funny thing, Gracie Moo. See you tomorrow, my lovely chum.

I know I've gone monosyllabic because my brain's now focusing on my *amazing plan* and I want to lie in the dark and run it through in my head until it's all joined up and making sense and I've visualized the whole thing happening and what I'm going to say. It makes doing stuff easier if I do that.

As I reach over to put my phone on the bedside table, there's another buzz.

Hey. See you at the shore tomorrow? :-)

It's not Anna. It's Gabe.

There's a little smiley face emoticon at the end—old-style, like the ones we used to send when we got our first phones. I don't reply, because I know I'm going to be there, and now I know he is too. I lie back against the pillows and plot tomorrow in my head until I fall asleep.

CHAPTER TWENTY-TWO

The house is still whispering creakily to itself when I get up. It's Saturday, the one morning of the week when nobody needs to go anywhere—except me. Even Withnail doesn't get up, but just opens one eye from the sofa and looks at me as I put my head through the sitting-room door to see if she wants breakfast.

The hall is quiet.

I make a coffee first, because I know that today I'm going to need maximum caffeine. I forgot to charge my phone after last night's middle-of-the-night conversation with Anna, so I leave it charging while I sit at the table listening to the hum of the lights and eating my toast. I even clean up the crumbs and put my plate in the sink.

My black jodhpurs are in the tumble dryer, and I pull them out in a tangle of school tights and Leah's tennis stuff, extracting them with a crackle of static. I put them on, then put on my favorite black T-shirt and hoodie. I loop my hair back in a ponytail and stick my beanie on top.

I pack my stuff and shove it down into my backpack. I don't feel hungry now, but I stick a packet of Penguin cookies in just in case I do later. My head is buzzing with plans already and I feel weirdly light-headed with excitement. I want it to be the afternoon, but I've got lots to do first.

GOING UP TO YARD—BACK BEFORE LUNCH.

I scribble a note on the back of one of the envelopes that's piled on the kitchen dresser and shove it on the table for Mum to see when she gets up.

I pull the front door closed behind me.

As I get onto my bike, I realize the sky is the strangest, brightest red I've ever seen. It rises like a weird bank of crimson behind the houses opposite, tinting the world pink. It's beautiful but strangely eerie. I'm glad when I hear the whirring and clinking of the milk truck as it turns into our street. The milkman waves an arm at the sky as he jumps out from the cab.

"Morning, love. Sailors take warning, eh?"

CHAPTER TWENTY-THREE

Mabel takes a step backward, the metal of her shoes scraping on the ancient cobbles of her stable floor. I pull the door toward me and slip inside, bolting it behind me. I bury my hands underneath her mane and place my cheek against the solid warmth of her neck, soaking up the sweetness of her scent. She feels like home. And the house doesn't feel like that anymore, so coming here makes me feel like I belong to something.

I take the soft brush and slip my hand through the strap that holds it in place, and I start grooming her in the quietness of the empty morning. I want her to look her absolute best. I spray her mane and tail with detangler and comb them through until they are silkily perfect. I clean her hooves and apply shiny black hoof oil to each one so they glisten.

By the time I'm finished, she's immaculate and I'm soaked with sweat, strands of my hair plastered to my forehead and my hoodie thrown to one side of the stable. I slip a day rug over Mabel in case she decides to do her usual trick of lying down in something disgusting when she's left to her own devices, and tie her up a net of hay to eat. She's not impressed. She wants out, but that will have to wait.

Beth, Polly's weekend cover, is mucking out the stables in the barn. I give her a wave as I fill a bucket of water for Mabel and haul it back over to her box.

The yard is coming to life now, the weekend riders arriving in their cars. During the week it's quiet most of the time, but when the weekends come this place becomes a hubbub with the radio playing and the jumping ponies being taken off to local competitions. I don't do any of that stuff because competing makes me feel sick with nerves, but I like watching. Sometimes I go along and help out. Freezing-cold fingers in huge, echoey indoor arenas, and the excitement of the jump-offs, and the bad burgers and the coffee in Styrofoam cups—it's amazing to be part of it but only on the sidelines. I like my horse stuff here at home. That's enough for me.

"All right, Grace? You riding today?" Beth pops a head through the door when she sees me sitting.

I've put the kettle on for coffee. I'm cleaning Mabel's bridle because I want it to look perfect for later, rubbing saddle soap in and shining the buckles and the metal of her bit. I've got her saddle balanced across my knees, ready to be done next.

"Later. I'm keeping her in this morning, though."

Beth raises her eyebrows. "You sure?"

"Yeah," I say, fastening the reins back together.

I know what Mabel's like when the wind is blowing, but I like it. She's like a kite on legs, darting and skipping unpredictably. But I can read her mind, and we fly together.

I go back to her stable, and she spins on her heels as she hears me approach and arches her head out of the stable door, nostrils flaring with excitement. *Is it time?* she asks me, her ears pricked forward, questing.

"Not yet, beautiful," I tell her, placing a hand on her neck. "Soon."

She harrumphs a snort of disgust and turns back to her hay net.

I leave Beth sitting on the sofa reading an ancient *Horse & Hound* magazine, and get back on my bike to go home—via Gabe's house.

I leave my bike balanced on the hedge outside and creep through the gate, holding my breath. There's a second where the metal hinges seem as if they're about to squeal in protest, but I manage to edge through sideways, so they quiet down again and I tiptoe up the path. I don't want to be caught in the act.

I bend down and a fluffy white cat appears out of nowhere and swirls its tail around my nose. I open the letterbox and carefully, silently, post the envelope through the door.

Later, when Gabe gets up, he'll find a retro *Doctor Who* DVD from me, and Marek will discover that I've found him a little blue TARDIS key ring of his own. I run on tiptoes down the path and back to the bike and cycle away, crossing my fingers that they haven't spotted me.

ooo

It's weird the way it feels when I'm excited about something. It's like I'm whirring with energy that comes from nowhere. The lights are brighter and sparklier, and the world seems sharper. I'm cycling, but it feels like no effort at all, and even the little hill that sometimes wears me out feels like nothing. My legs are full of power. Today I feel like I could do anything, be anyone. I'm flying like Mabel. We're connected. Today is going to be a good day. The stars have aligned.

ooo

"Hello, darling," says Mum, opening the door as I clatter onto the front steps, leaving my bike lying across them, the wheel still spinning. "You can't leave that there."

"I'm just going back out once I've had a shower and something to eat," I explain, darting past her.

"Not with that lying there," she says, catching my arm and pulling me back, half laughing as she does so, and pushing me from behind out onto the step. "At least put it around the side. If you break the postie's ankles, I'll be the one getting sued."

"Fair enough," I say, and wheel it around the side.

Inside, the house smells of freshly baked something. Leah's in the kitchen with oven gloves on, doing crocodile impressions to an un-amused Withnail, whose tail is twitching in irritation. There's no sign of Eve. This pleases me. My mood is good and I don't want the sight of her face ruining it.

"I made *pain au chocolat*," says Leah, waving her still-gloved hands with a flourish at the kitchen counter. "Well, I assembled them from a can, but you know what I mean."

"Ooh, yum." I reach forward to get one, but she smacks my hand away.

"Too hot. Hands off the merchandise."

"Fine," I say. "Don't eat them all before I get out of the shower."

"What are you up to today?" Leah says, and her voice is weirdly loud, as if she wants to be overheard.

I frown at her. "Nothing much." I don't want to tell anyone my idea. If I do, it might break the spell.

"Right," says Leah, still in the same foghorn voice. "I'm going out with Malia later."

"Not Meg?"

"No, I'm having a sleepover at Malia's house."

"Why are you yelling?"

"I was just going to ask the same question," says Mum, coming into the room and picking up a *pain au chocolat* and biting into it before Leah can protest. "So, you're having a sleepover at Malia's?"

"Yep." Leah nods.

"I'll give you a lift over." Mum's talking through a mouthful of burning hot pastry, so her voice is all muffled. "I'm going out to the cinema with Eve."

Leah shoots me a one-second glance. "'S fine," she says, wiping the counter with a cloth. "Malia's mum said she'd collect me on the way back from the shops later. Save you the worry."

Mum swallows and gives Leah a smile. "You are an angel."

ooo

I run upstairs two at a time. Some days feel like they should have a soundtrack. I'm humming as I turn on the shower and head for the bedroom to get my stuff.

"Grace, will you NOT leave the shower running when you're not in it," I hear the voice of doom yelling from the hall.

"Sorry," I shout back.

I'm not really sorry. I like the bathroom when it's all full of steam and smoggy and thick so you go in and it's like being in the jungle. I hate getting in when it's cold and you freeze for ages before our not-working-properly boiler finally deigns to let you have some hot water.

I stand under the hot needles of the shower for ages, letting them burn into my scalp, washing and conditioning my hair and scrubbing my face until it feels squeaky smooth.

I emerge as Grace 2.0, the shiny, perfect edition.

I'm putting on makeup, but not too much because if I put on loads there will be *where are* you *going?* comments, and I don't want comments. Or questions. So I paint on some eyeliner, and when my wings are perfect first time, I give up a little prayer of thanks to the gods of makeup. When your eyeliner goes right, you just know you're going to have a good day.

I smooth some defuzzing stuff through my hair (which is pointless because it's going to be under a hat and also because, let's face it, fuzz is what my hair does best, and even industrial-strength defuzzer is no match for it) and put on some red-tinted lip-balm stuff.

I'm not going to wear jodhpurs. I put on my black jeans and my *Doctor Who* T-shirt and my black fuzzy cardigan. When I go downstairs, I wait until there's nobody in the kitchen and shove a box of matches and as much food as I can manage into my backpack. I sneak into the garage and stuff the chocolate and marshmallows and cookies into my bag too. It feels a bit like I'm on a Famous Five adventure.

I'm ready.

CHAPTER TWENTY-FOUR

t's like riding a coiled spring. We skitter sideways out of the yard and Beth, closing the gate to the outdoor school, raises her eyebrows again.

"She's going to be full of it in this weather," she warns. I grin and wave a hand in acknowledgment and we surge forward. Mabel is bursting to gallop and leap and soar and fly, but we clatter onto the tarmac in a barely contained walk. Her shoes tap out her irritation in staccato bursts.

"Almost there," I tell her. We can ride down the shore road and along the beach path to town, and she can stretch her legs on the foot-path there.

It's harder than I thought it would be, riding in jeans. The stirrup leathers pinch at the insides of my legs where the jodhpurs have protective padding, and my cardigan's flapping in the wind, which hasn't eased up. The backpack is banging on my back and heavy on my shoulders. I sort of wish I'd brought a coat or something to keep me warm, but I want to look nice. Not weird. And it's going to be amazing. Nobody else there will have a *horse*. Holly Carmichael doesn't have a horse.

We pass the Spar and wait at the traffic lights, Mabel pawing the ground impatiently as we stand with a little yellow Volkswagen Beetle waiting for the lights to change. She's good in traffic, but in this mood she wants to go and go and go, and red lights aren't part of her plans.

"Look, Mummy, a unicorn," says a little girl in a stroller, pointing as she crosses in front of us.

"No, it's just a horse, sweetie," says her mum, and I glare at her for breaking the spell. She's not just a horse. She's magic and fire and she could be a unicorn if she wanted to. I give the little girl a smile and hope that she can read my mind. The lights switch to green and Mabel soars forward into a trot. We make our way past the squat little bungalows that line the shore road, and cross over onto the beach path. The grass is bleached gray-blue with sunlight and sea wind, and the tide is far, far out, miles from the shore. In the distance where the sea touches the sky, dark towers of clouds are bunched together. The salt marsh that stretches out toward the sea looks empty, but as we pass, a flock of birds wheels up into the sky, their wings beating as one, the air stirring in a whoosh around them.

I can't let the reins loose and let Mabel go, because the path is dotted with dog walkers. I'd forgotten they'd be everywhere. It's why we don't ride down on the beach—that and the broken glass, which lurks, waiting to bite, in hummocks of grass. So I keep the reins tight and Mabel tosses her head up and down in irritation, the metal of her bit jangling, her nostrils fire red.

I'd check my phone, but I feel safer with both hands on the reins when she's in this mood. My excitement of earlier is being engulfed by a gnawing sense that I'm making a mistake, but it's too late to do anything about it. I keep going as Mabel's frustration rises. We dance past dog walkers and joggers until the wooden climbing frame of the shore park can be seen on the left, behind the wall where the go-karts circle around and around all summer.

I almost want to get off and lead her across the road, but I don't. I don't want to chicken out. This is the moment I've planned. I try to take a deep breath, but I feel like my lungs are made of lead.

"Mabel!"

And it's worth it then, because when we clatter along the path and Anna sees us she looks so impressed and proud and delighted that I'm glad I've done it.

"Whoa," says Archie, and he carefully places his scooter down on the ground, so it doesn't make a noise. I am grateful for this because Mabel is virtually vibrating with excitement, and emitting small, brisk snorts. "You've got an actual horse."

And everyone crowds around, Jacob and Tom and Jamie and Archie, and then there's Gabe, and his cousin Marek with wide eyes, and Gabe looks up at me with his sparkly brown eyes and I think he's impressed. And even though I know I shouldn't be pleased he's impressed, I still feel pleased. And a lot like this must be how it feels to be Holly Carmichael and be the center of attention when you walk into a room and everyone looks at you.

Plus, I'm quite high up, so everyone's looking up at me and circling Mabel, and I sort of feel like one of those statues you see in the middle of London, except my horse isn't standing still in a noble and obedient manner.

"OW," says Archie. "She's on my bloody foot. Grace?"

I ease Mabel sideways so she steps off, and I slide out of the saddle, running up the stirrups automatically.

"She's amazing," says Jacob. "I can't believe you've got an actual horse as a pet."

"She's not exactly a pet," I begin, and I realize Gabe is laughing at Jacob and looking at me and I feel like I've discovered the secret to life. I knew when I figured out that the boys only took their scooters and stuff to the park so they had something to do with themselves that there had to be an equivalent. I'd just have to take Mabel everywhere I go. She might find it a bit of a squash fitting into seats at the cinema, but I could work something out. It was worth it to feel like this.

"She's really soft," says Marek, running a cautious hand down her neck. I'm glad I spent so long grooming her this morning. "And thank you for my gift."

He smiles at me and I smile back. And Gabe does a thing where his eyebrows sort of crinkle up his forehead and he smiles too and says, "Yeah, that was a nice surprise. Thank you." And he looks pleased, and I feel like today is officially Going Very Well.

"I can't believe you've brought her here," says Anna, in a low voice. "Your mum would literally *explode* if she knew."

"She doesn't need to know, does she?" I reply. "Anyway, she's too busy with her new best friend."

Mabel jerks my arm up, nudging me impatiently. She drags me across the path to the grass that tufts up beside the swings.

"Do you think you should have a horse in here, young lady?" says an old man with a walking stick. He settles down on the bench nearby. "She looks like a bit of a wild one."

Mabel pulls her head up at that, with a piece of grass hanging out of the side of her mouth like a farmer. She looks into the far distance as if she can see something we can't, and lets out a shrill whinny. It sounds weirdly out of place in among all the tarmac and metal of the park.

"Is she okay?" says Anna, looking at me anxiously. "She looks a bit—"

"She's fine," I say, closing her down. Although I'm not sure she is, and I'm not sure what I'm supposed to do now that the initial excitement has passed. Archie's picked up his scooter and is spinning one of the wheels with a finger. Gabe's standing nearby. I notice that the collar on his plaid shirt is sticking up at one side and I wonder what it would feel like to reach across and fix it. And then I feel myself going weirdly fizzy inside when I realize that not very long ago I had my hand inside that same shirt and I could feel the muscles on his back underneath his T-shirt. It feels like something that happened to someone else. But he sent me a message and asked if I was going to be here, and I *am* here.

"Anyone fancy going down the arcade to get a hot dog?" Tom, who has been looking slightly edgy, shoves his phone back in his pocket. I don't think he likes horses. In fact, I think he's a bit nervous. Mabel stamps her foot, kicking at an irritation on her stomach. I don't want things to change, but they are. It's like someone's blurred a picture with a filter.

"What's she doing?" Tom steps back a bit farther. I can see alarm on his face, his mouth set in a flat line. "Is she all right?"

"She's fine," I say. "Anna, did you bring the stuff?"

"It's here." She picks up a big Sainsbury's bag.

"You don't need hot dogs," Anna explains to Tom. "We've got stuff for a beach barbecue."

Tom curls his lip slightly. "Seriously?"

"I've got chocolate and marshmallows," I say brightly. I realize I'm sounding like a children's television presenter again and I can feel the awkwardness descending.

"Oh, well, if you've got *chocolate and marshmallows*," says Tom, with a look that might be serious or mocking—I can't tell—"that changes everything. Fire it up."

"And maybe someone can have a ride on Mabel if they like?" I hear my mouth saying. I have no idea why.

Anna shoots me a look. It's a look that says *this is not a good plan*.

I look back at her and shrug. It's out there now and maybe nobody else will hear. Or they'll just think I'm joking.

Anna shakes her head slightly, frowning, and I'm not sure what the expression on her face says. And then a gust of wind blows her hair across her face so I can't see it anyway.

And Gabe's cousin Marek says—

"I would love to."

And he smiles at me and I think that maybe it'll be okay. There's a whistling sound as the wind gets trapped in the metal of the swings, and it makes Mabel stand taller, ears pricked, focusing. I shake her reins gently, trying to bring her attention back to me. One ear flicks in my direction but switches back again.

"Come on, then," says Archie. "I've got to see this."

"Not here," says Anna. She's chewing the inside of her lip.

Jamie says something, but I don't quite catch it, and I realize that I'm crashing after the excitement of this morning. This happens. It always happens. I don't want it to. I'm not going to let it.

"I said why don't you take her over to the beach path?" Jamie looks at me, the expression on his face slightly odd, as if he can't work out why I didn't hear him the first time. I hear my heart thudding in my ears and there's a sort of blurring of children on swings and whistling wind and I hear the *tickticktick* of the chain of Jacob's bike as it spins, and Anna's saying something because her mouth is moving but the sounds aren't connecting with my head and I smell vanilla ice cream from a little child on the baby swings across the way.

"Let's take her over, then," I say, and my voice sounds brittle and louder than I meant it to. "Come on, Mabel." I turn and she follows me like a kite in the wind.

"Grace," says Anna warningly.

"It's fine." I don't catch her eye. This is what cool people do. They take risks; they do exciting things. It's not like I'm downing a bottle of vodka and jumping off the pier.

"You okay?" says Gabe, and he catches my elbow as we stand waiting on the pavement, me and my horse and a bag full of sweating sausages and my best friend and her not-yet-boyfriend on a scooter and our friends with their long legs folded up on short little BMX bikes and Gabe—my I-don't-know-what—and his cousin Marek from Warsaw, who wants to get on my horse and ride on the beach and have an adventure.

I turn to look at him and I realize how ridiculous I must look with my riding hat on and I wonder if my ears are sticking out of the sides, because sometimes they do. And I notice that he's got a little constellation of freckles under his left eye. And I look down at his hand, which is still sort of cupping my elbow in a way that feels kind.

"Fine," I say brightly. Because I don't know how to say all the other things.

We cross the road, horse and people and bikes and scooters and noise and jumble, and one by one pass through the little metal gateway that leads from the promenade down to the beach path, and then we stop on the grass. The air smells of wet sand and dirty seaweed and all the things that people don't mention when they dream of living by the sea, the things we just take for granted. And the wind is whipping across us. I can't work out whether the spots I'm feeling on my face are sea spray or the beginnings of rain, and I wish again that I weren't just wearing a cardigan and a T-shirt. A shiver passes through me.

Anna pulls the barbecue out of her bag and I throw her the matches, which are in the pocket of my backpack. I watch her squatting down to try to light the corner of it, and Archie cupping his hands around to stop the wind from the sea blowing out the flame, and eventually there's a flare of light and they catch. Mabel snorts in horror, pulling back against me so the reins, wrapped around my hand, tighten.

"Can I give you this?" I say to Gabe. I pass him the backpack full of food so I can hold on to Mabel with both hands. "It's got the food in it," I explain, pointing at the zip.

"Here," says Anna, "I'll take it."

Everyone is sort of milling around and the tiny little aluminum barbecue is not quite the focal point I imagined.

Tom is looking at something on his phone and I catch him saying he might just head back, and asking Archie if he wants to head up to the skate park. Archie shakes his head, though—he's helping Anna rip open a packet of squashed-looking sausages.

"What's this?"

I feel my stomach disappearing through my feet and onto the ground. I'd recognize that voice anywhere. I turn around, and Holly's standing there, legs akimbo in a short denim skirt, her hair pushed back from her face with a pair of sunglasses. She's got something in her hand, and I realize it's a cheap plastic kite with a scrunched-up-looking SpongeBob on the front.

"We're having a beach party," I say, "and you're not actually invited."

My heart thumps really hard then, and I feel a bit sick. But she's rude all the time, and it's about time someone treated her the same way she treats me.

Tom mutters something out of the side of his mouth to Jacob, who bursts out laughing.

"It's a free country," says Holly. And she winks at Gabe.

And then—because somehow I'd forgotten—I turn to Mabel, who is something she wants and can't have, just like Gabe is, and I run a hand along her mane and glare at Holly and don't say anything.

"Do you want to ride her now?" I say, turning to Marek.

"Please," he says, and he smiles at me. I lead her up to the edge of the beach path, leaving Anna and Archie poking at the barbecue.

And—because everyone always says that you can't sneeze around here without the whole town knowing about it—a battered little red car drives past as we're standing there and I see Polly's face in the window looking out at me and her expression says, *What the hell are you doing, Grace?*

And I half wish she'd stop the car and end this because I've messed up, and there's a horrible feeling in the air, but it's a little late.

I take a look at Marek's legs—he's a bit taller than me—and I adjust the stirrups so they'll fit. I check the girth to make sure the saddle isn't going to slip when he gets on.

"Here," I say, and I hand him my hat, because even when I'm taking risks I like to follow the approved safety procedures.

Marek puts it on his head, and Archie grins at him and taps his own head. "Cool, man. We're twins."

Archie's skating helmet is so much a part of him that I forget he's got an actual head under there.

I hear the crack of Holly's gum and realize she's standing close by, watching. Her eyes on me make my neck feel prickly and hot.

Mabel is standing stock-still, looking out across the huge expanse of muddy sand that makes up our beach. In the distance I can see the gray-white frill of water, almost on the horizon, which indicates that the tide is coming in.

I turn to Marek, who is stroking Mabel's neck. "Do you know how to get on?" She's transfixed by something, her focus on the middle distance, and he might as well be a fly for all the difference his affection is making. Her muscles are taut and tense, and I can see the veins crisscross underneath the seal-smoothness of her skin. She looks beautiful, but half-wild, like a white horse of the seas come to land. The wind blows her silver mane up in the air.

"Can you help me?"

"Sure," I say.

"Grace," says Anna, appearing from nowhere.

"Will you hold Mabel's head?" I turn to her and ignore the expression on her face. Her face is sort of rigid, and her mouth is held in a straight line. But she takes hold of the bridle on either side of Mabel's cheeks, keeping her steady, and I tell her to keep Mabel's head still while I give Marek a leg up.

"Here," says Gabe, and he steps forward. "I'll do it."

I smile a small thank-you smile at him. I'd forgotten that he'd had experience with horses.

"Lift your foot up behind you," he says to Marek. "Take hold of the saddle, here."

And there's a pause for a second as the sounds of raucous laughter and shrieks blow on the wind from behind us, and I turn to see what it is just as Gabe takes Marek's bent leg in his hands.

Mabel tenses slightly and Anna shoots me a look of alarm.

I feel Gabe stepping back behind me and I feel the thinness of leather reins in my hands and the rush of the wind in my ears and Mabel jumps sideways, suddenly, with a snort.

Holly and her friends laugh loudly.

"It's quite high up here, isn't it?" Marek wobbles, still holding on to the top of the saddle as he's been instructed. Gabe takes a step forward.

"Are you actually going to go for a ride?" says Jacob, and he reverses his BMX back off the path to clear the way and I look at Anna, who shakes her head slightly, and I say, "Sure."

And again I take a moment to process the words before they make it into my head, and by the time I nod back at Gabe, enough time has passed that I think he's looking at me strangely and I wonder if he thinks I don't understand something. But it's not him—it's the wind and my panic, which is rising, blowing up and up.

"Shh, Mabel," I whisper, but the wind whips the words away as I chant them.

"Be good, be quiet, be nice—"

"Ready?" says Gabe.

And we start to walk along the path. I'm holding on to Mabel's head and Marek says something and I turn to hear what he's said because with the wind and my brain melting I can't catch it without concentrating. And in that second when my attention turns from her to him I hear a shriek and see Holly Carmichael and her cronies running along the beach, laughing and pointing, waving their arms in the air, and there's a flutter as something yellow flies past my head, carried by the wind, something plastic and colorful and flappy, and it flies between me and Marek and wraps itself for a second around Mabel's head and she pulls away.

I try to grab the reins back, but I'm torn in that second because I can feel Marek slipping sideways. I reach forward to grab him so he doesn't fall, and Mabel throws her head in the air, snorting again with fear. I see the white of her eye as she throws her head sideways, tossing it up to get the thing off.

As it flies up, I realize it's Holly's kite. It sails up into the sky.

And Marek falls then, landing backward on me with a force that knocks my breath out in a huff of surprise. Mabel takes a sideways leap and, realizing she's not being held anymore, she bolts, and it's like everything just stops.

I can't move. Marek's half pinning me to the ground and I feel sick, as if I've been punched in the stomach, and everyone is flapping and screaming at Holly, at Mabel, at me—

"Grace, I *knew* this was a bad idea!" Anna screams at me, looming over me, her face all twisted with anger.

Oh God, come back, come back.

Come back.

I scramble up from underneath Marek and watch in horror as Mabel shies again at a pile of rocks on the side of the path, jumping like a startled cat and then pecking slightly as her leg gets caught in the reins, which have come loose over her head, and I can see her then broken and lying with her legs smashed and I know I've killed her and I've made this happen and everyone is still screaming and Holly is still shrieking and it's all my fault. I shouldn't have brought her here.

So I run.

CHAPTER TWENTY-FIVE

t's raining now.

The wind is battering against the roof of the seaside shelter and the rain is dripping down in front of me. I'm cold inside and out. The clouds are so low that it feels as if it's getting dark. I feel as if I'm shivering inside and my teeth won't stop chattering.

My phone keeps buzzing in my pocket, but I can't look at it.

"You all right, my love?" says an old man. I realize he's the same one we saw in the park earlier. I recognize his walking stick with a carved wooden fox on the handle. "Got caught in a shower, did you?"

I look at him, but I can't make my mouth make the right noises. My face is numb. It feels as if the world is being torn away in strips around me. I feel as if I'm in a black hole.

"Best place for you," he nods. "Keep dry. It'll be fine again soon enough."

I look down at the ground. He splashes away along the pavement.

The phone is buzzing continually now. I want it to go away. I want it all to go away. I've broken everything.

I pull it out of my pocket. Maybe the best thing to do is throw it away.

Maybe the best thing to do is throw myself away.

I catch a glimpse of the screen.

It's Polly.

Something—guilt, panic, or the fact that I'm a bit scared of her—makes me answer.

"Where the hell are you?"

She roars so loudly that I half expect to turn around and find her standing behind me.

"I—"

"I've got your bloody horse here, Grace, and she's . . ." There's a pause and I feel a wave of sickness and something else pass over me, something so strong that I feel as if I could die of it if I lie down here for long enough.

"I'm—" I try to speak, but the words are held back by a knot in my throat that makes it impossible.

"She's fine—no thanks to *you*," Polly yells, "but you better get your backside down here right now. Your mother's out in the car driving around trying to find you and I've got the vet on the way."

She's not dead.

I don't know how it's happened, but she's not dead. I look back at the phone screen—Polly's ended the call now, and it's full of a million notifications that I can't even process, but . . . she's not dead. I put my hands against my cheeks, which feel weird. They're rock hard with sadness and panic and I feel the cold of my skin.

She's not dead.

I feel a rush of relief. But then I remember all the faces of my friends and the screaming and the yelling and the chaos and that I just left them. And I know I won't ever be able to face them again.

CHAPTER TWENTY-SIX

start running along the coast road toward the stables. I can't fix what's happened, but I can do something about Mabel. My heart is pounding in my ears and my stomach is aching.

I don't stop, even when I start stumbling because my legs are shaking and it feels as if my lungs are going to explode. I just keep on going, imagining the panic Mabel felt when she was running away, forcing myself to carry on.

I don't hear the beeping at first, and when the car passes I don't even recognize it. Mum stops in the middle of the road—she's got the door open and the hazard lights all flashing and she runs toward me and throws herself at me and squeezes me in the middle of the road. Another car passes by and I hear a voice, distorted by the wind, yelling something out of the window.

Mum pulls back and looks at me.

"Grace." And I can see she's been crying and her face is all white. "Oh God, Grace. What were you thinking? Where did you go?"

And I just look at her because I don't have the words to make sense of what I'm feeling.

She puts her arm around my shoulder and it's uncomfortable, but I don't shrug it off, and she sort of steers me into the car and shuts the door and runs around and gets in.

"Fasten your seat belt." She starts the car and drives away before she fastens hers.

"This is my fault," she says. "Shit," she adds, as she pulls the car across the junction onto the shore road toward the stables. A truck blares its horn at her as it misses us by a second.

"And where the hell is your father when all this is going on?" she shouts, banging her hand on the steering wheel as we get stuck at the traffic light. "It's my fault. I took my eye off the ball."

I don't say anything. I look out at the Spar and remember riding past and how it felt when I was soaring and Mabel was flying and how we were amazing.

We pull into the stable yard and for a second I hesitate. I can't bring myself to open the car door and see what's happened.

Mum comes around and pulls it open for me.

"She's fine, honey," she says, and extends a hand to pull me out of my seat. I feel like everything is made of rusty metal. I walk like a robot toward Mabel's box, passing the vet's Land Rover as I go.

I don't want to look inside.

"Grace," says Polly. She looks through the half-open stable door and her face looks—I don't know. I don't know the look on her face. It's not one I recognize.

"Julia." Polly's squatting by the vet's side, but she reaches across and pushes the door ajar to let us in and Mabel turns to look at me and she whickers a greeting. I feel tears rolling down my cheeks and they're hot.

"Grace, I'm sorry I screamed at you."

Polly runs a hand through her hair so it sticks up wonkily and her expression changes to one I do recognize. She looks at me kindly. She wobbles slightly and puts out a hand on the floor to balance herself.

Mabel heaves a huge sigh, blowing through her nostrils, and shakes herself with a scraping of hooves on the cobbled stable floor.

"She's a bit battered and bruised"—the vet straightens up and turns to look at Mum—"but nothing a bit of TLC won't fix." She runs a hand along Mabel's back, and Mabel gives an involuntary shudder, her tail swishing.

"That's good—her reflexes are fine," she says, and smiles at me. "Have you two been in the wars?"

"Something like that," says Mum. She looks at me and frowns.

"Looks like one of you needs a hot bath and the other a large gin and tonic." The vet taps something into her phone. "I've put a couple of stitches in the gash in her thigh—it was clean, so it should heal up without much of a mark."

"And box rest?" says Polly, putting a hand on Mabel's neck. I still haven't reached out to her. I feel too guilty.

"Keep her in tonight, but I'd get her out in the morning—have you got an isolation paddock?"

Polly nods. "I can shift a couple of the ponies around and put her somewhere safe." She ruffles Mabel's long mane gently. "We don't want you getting in any more trouble."

Mum holds the stable door open and then follows the vet, asking something about the bill. I realize that it'll be enormous—call out on a weekend is huge, and Mabel's had stitches. I feel another wave of sick dread washing over me.

"Right, then," says Polly. And she smiles at me kindly. "Let's get this one bedded down for the night."

I reach a hand across, holding it out carefully. Mabel puts her muzzle gently into it and breathes a huff of warm breath through my fingers, the fine hairs of her whiskers tickling my skin. I could just collapse on the floor and cry forever, but my face is still stony and unmoving. Inside I want to scream. It's too big to let it out, too scary. I need to put it to one side and I can be upset later, when I'm home, when I know I've done everything I can.

There isn't time to feel cold anymore. I get a couple of bags of shavings from the barn and rip the plastic coverings open, scattering them around to make Mabel's bed as soft and warm as I can. I bank up the sides so if she does lie down there won't be a draft creeping in from under the stable door.

Mum slips back into the stable. "How's she doing?"

"Good," says Polly. "She was lucky."

"I can't thank you enough, Polly." Mum turns to look at me, putting her purse back in her bag. I feel a bit sick thinking about the bill. I add it to my things-to-think-about-later list and turn away, fixing the handles on Mabel's water bucket so they're facing the wall neatly.

Polly looks at me for a moment and I cast my eyes down.

"What on earth were you thinking?"

"I . . ." I have to stop for a moment and swallow because the wave of everything is threatening to engulf me again. "I just—"

Mum shakes her head. "Thank God you were there." She reaches out to Polly, taking her hand and squeezing it.

"It's fine." Polly shakes her head. "The minute I saw the lot of them crossing the road I told Mel to pull up on Carol Street. We were walking down to give you a scolding—"

I look up for a moment. She looks fierce but kind at the same time.

"I could tell that it was going to end in some sort of disaster. And the next second, Mabel comes hurtling along the beach path like a bat out of hell."

I close my eyes because I don't want to picture it, but when I do I flash back to standing there, watching Mabel careering along the path.

"Honestly, Polly, I can't—I just—if you hadn't been there . . ." Mum trails off.

Mabel gives a harrumphing sigh and clops over to her water. She takes a drink and looks at me, her eyes huge and liquid brown. She's got a dressing on her one foreleg and some scrapes on the other, and the gash the vet has stitched makes me feel queasy. And guilty. I did this. I start shaking again. It starts inside, and within moments my knees are trembling so much that Mum reaches out and puts her arms around me.

"Take her home, Julia. I'm staying in the apartment above the tack room tonight; I'll keep an eye on Mabel."

"I'm fine," I protest through chattering teeth.

"You've had a shock," says Polly firmly. "You need a hot cup of tea and a big sleep."

"But I need to be here for her."

"Polly's right, honey," says Mum. I try to protest, but she's squeezed me more tightly so that when I speak it's into a mouthful of her coat.

"I promise you I'll call if there's any problem." Polly puts an arm over Mabel's neck. "Look, she's telling you to go home and get a rest. We'll see you in the morning."

"Are you sure?"

I'm suddenly so tired that I feel as if I could sleep forever.

"Promise."

"Polly, I can't thank you enough for this. I—that's just—I don't even have the words," begins Mum.

"No need," says Polly, shaking her head.

I don't have the words either. And I can't get my mouth to work. It's like my face is frozen.

"Thank you," I say, and I want to say so much more, but those two words cost me all the energy I have left.

I allow myself to be propelled toward the car by Mum. My legs are leaden and stiff. I'm still shaking.

"Right," says Mum, switching on the engine. "That is more than enough drama for one night."

It's dark now and the headlights shine over the little paddock where the ponies live as we turn out of the yard. Tomorrow Mabel will be allowed out there to stretch her legs.

"I'm sorry," says Mum, as we pull onto the shore road. "This is all my fault. I've been so busy thinking about myself that I've forgotten you girls."

I turn to look at her, but she's staring ahead, both hands on the wheel. I'm not sure where she gets that idea from. We drive past the park and the dip in the road and I close my eyes again because I don't want to picture it. I've almost killed my horse and my attempts at making myself a popular like Holly have resulted in this. I'm sitting alone in the car, and I've got nobody.

"Things are going to change," says Mum as we turn up toward home. The indicator light ticks and I tap my finger and thumb in time with it to reassure myself. But I'm so far past counting or tapping or humming or anything that would normally reset my brain. I feel as if I'm falling into a dark tunnel, and I still can't stop shaking.

"When we get Leah back from Meg's house tomorrow, I'm doing proper Sunday lunch and we're going to have a serious chat."

I press my head sideways against the cool of the glass, feeling the strands of my hair prickle on my skin.

"Nearly there."

She reaches across and squeezes my knee. It's supposed to comfort me, I know, but it's just more information when my brain's already overloaded.

We pull into the drive. All I want to do is make it upstairs, climb under my covers, and sleep for a week. I shuffle in ahead of Mum.

Leah's left her *Adventure Time* satchel lying on the doorstep.

I step over it. The door is ajar.

I push it open, turning as I do so. "Did you leave the door open?" I say to Mum over my shoulder.

"No, I didn't." Mum's face goes pale.

CHAPTER TWENTY-SEVEN

There's a sweetish, sickly sort of smell as I walk into the hall. I can't place it.

"Grace—" Mum puts a hand on my arm, holding me back. She pushes past, shoving open the door into the sitting room.

"Leah!"

I don't get it—

I step forward into the room, and as I do the smell gets stronger. I cover my mouth and nose with my hand.

"*Leah.*"

Mum's on her knees beside the sofa.

That's when I see her.

Leah is lying on her side, and her lips are bluish pale. One arm sticks out from underneath her, the fingers extended as if she's reaching out to stroke Withnail or take something. But there's a trail of silvery-green vomit, which drips down from her mouth, over her arm, and pools on the wooden floor.

"Oh God, oh God." Mum's shaking her, and she's starting to cry. *"Leah."*

I can't move. I just stand there watching. It's like my brain has run out of processing space. First Mabel and now Leah. And where are her friends? They must have known she was here.

There's a groan from the sofa.

"Leah!" shouts Mum. "Can you hear me? Sweetheart. Darling—it's Mummy." She pushes at Leah's inert shape again.

"Grace!" She turns to me, her eyes flashing. *"Call an ambulance."*

I can't.

"I can't."

"What?"

I—I just can't pick up the phone and speak to—

"Call an ambulance. Now."

I shake my head and start walking backward. I bump into the wall and shake my head again.

"No."

I can't speak to a stranger now. I can't make my words come. I can feel myself sliding down the wall.

"Do I have to do everything myself?" Mum's still shaking Leah with one hand and pulling the phone out of her bag with the other. She looks at me with absolute hatred. I can see it burning in her eyes.

I close mine. I can't do any more of anything. The relief that Mabel is okay has been instantly replaced by gut-wrenching fear. I can't lose my sister. I can't lose Leah. I feel frozen, like a hideous gargoyle, gripped in terror.

"Ambulance," I hear Mum saying. There's a sort of muffled groaning from Leah, and as Mum's talking she coughs.

I open my eyes and watch as Leah spews a never-ending fountain of vomit all over Mum. It pours over her arm and down into her bag, splashing all over the floor. And Mum just leans forward, dripping, and pulls Leah into her arms, and starts rubbing her back. And all I can think is that I knew she wasn't going to a sleepover with Malia, and I knew she was hanging around with Lily Carmichael, and I let this happen. And now I'm going to lose her too, and I can't bear it.

I watch as with her free hand Mum fiddles with the phone.

"Lisa?"

I listen as she explains to Anna's mum that Leah's sick, that she needs a massive favor. There's nodding and then Mum starts crying.

And then there's a knock at the door. Something makes me stand up, and I pull the sitting-room door open.

"All right, love?" A paramedic in green and white smiles at me. He's got a kind face.

And another one follows. She's wearing a bright waistcoat and she pushes past, into the room. I step backward out of it and sit on the stairs in the hall, waiting. After what might have been moments, or maybe ages—I don't know—they come back with a trolley thing and I watch as Leah is rolled out of the front door toward an ambulance, which is waiting outside. I don't even know if she's alive. She's just strapped there and there's a weird sort of urgency in everyone's voice and I can't understand what the paramedic says through the radio but it sounds wrong. Wrong and scary and dark and—I don't want this to be happening.

"Oh God," says Mum as Lisa arrives. She pulls her bag onto her shoulder.

Lisa gives her a quick hug on the doorstep and I watch them both wipe away tears.

"Hello, my lovely," says Lisa, turning to me. She's given Mum a last touch on the shoulder as she rushes off to get into the back of the ambulance, where my little sister is lying, blue and covered in vomit.

And then something happens.

My eyes start leaking tears, and they roll down my cheeks. I try to bat them away with the backs of my hands, but they just pour over the tops and through my fingers and down over my T-shirt. All

I can think of is Leah's deathly pale face and if I hadn't been trying to impress everyone I would have been home and then Leah wouldn't have been alone. And this would never have happened. I caused all of this.

And Anna's mum—who smells of flowery things and different shampoo I don't recognize and is round, and soft, and kind—sits on her knees in front of me at the foot of the stairs and she puts her arms around me and the tears leak out of me and all over her and she doesn't seem to mind at all.

After a little while she sits back on her heels for a moment, and pulls her phone out of the back pocket of her jeans. I pick at the fluff on the stair carpet until I have a little ball of it in my hand as she reads a text, then looks at me with a soft smile. She's got the same eyes as Anna, but crinkly at the sides.

"Your mum says they're doing a few tests, but they think Leah's going to be fine."

I nod. Which is surprisingly hard when you feel as if you're made of stone.

"They're going to keep her in," Anna's mum continues, "and just look after her a bit, make sure she's got some fluids. She's going to be feeling a bit rough for a couple of days."

She stands, extending a hand to pull me up from the stairs. I let her help me and feel her hand wrapping around mine, warm and strong and capable. And it makes me think fleetingly of Anna and I feel unspeakably sad. I ran away from everyone and everything and they must all hate me for what I did. I swallow and it's like a huge ball of lead passes down my throat and settles in my stomach.

"I think we'll get you up to bed. You go and pop on some pj's. I'll get you a hot water bottle. Okay, darling?"

I nod. I want to ask if Anna's okay and where she is and why she didn't come too, but I can guess the answer. If she didn't hate me for what happened, she'd be here. So I just keep my mouth closed and I wait politely until I can get into my room and under my covers and then I can just stay there forever.

And I realize the sickly sweet smell that's filling the house is cider. Well, cider and puke.

Withnail is curled up on my bed. It looks so normal, like nothing has changed. I expected to walk in and find that the bed was burned and all the bookshelves were upside down and the chaos that was happening outside would have altered everything, but my bed is still unmade and yesterday's clothes are still on the floor. The book I was reading when I couldn't sleep last night is facedown on the carpet, and there's a half-drunk coffee sitting on the bedside table.

"Let me take that downstairs," says Lisa. She picks it up and a couple of other glasses and a plate, and stacks them together. "You girls," she says, and smiles a funny sort of smile. "I'll be back in five minutes. Do you want to hop in the shower and warm up?"

I shake my head. I don't even want to get changed. The idea of peeling off these layers seems impossibly hard. I sit down on the bed and begin, not because I want to, but because I know if I don't when she gets back I'll have to have the conversation all over again.

Withnail rubs her face across my hands as I'm pulling off my socks. She's purring and slinking around in circles. I pick her up for a moment and bury my face in her soft, warm-smelling fur. Then my brain flashes a picture of Mabel standing, legs cut and scarred, in her stable. I caused that. I'm not an animal lover. If I were, I wouldn't have let that happen. I don't deserve her, and I don't deserve Withnail. I put her down on the ground and pull off my jeans.

"Here you are—I found two hot water bottles. Fluffy ones. I've had a call from your mum, and Leah's in the ward. She's sleeping, and she's doing fine."

I feel ashamed. Anna's family is so nice and normal and everything happens the way it's supposed to. And somehow—I don't know how—one minute our house was the same every day and everything was boring. Now it feels like the whole family is falling apart.

"I'll pop them in there," says Lisa, and she pulls back the covers and tucks one hot water bottle at the foot of the bed, and another up by my pillow. She puts a hand on my shoulder and looks at me, her eyes—Anna's eyes—kind. "You've had more than enough to deal with today, Grace. You, and your mum, and Leah—all of you. You need to sleep."

It's like she can tell that my brain won't stop whirring.

"I'm going down to make you a hot chocolate. Get under those covers. No arguments."

I pull on a pair of pajamas that are stuffed under my pillow and climb under the covers. I know I'm not going to sleep tonight, no matter what she says. There's no way I could.

CHAPTER TWENTY-EIGHT

There's a second when I wake up when everything is normal. I reach over, blurrily, for my phone, but it's not on the bedside table or under my pillow. Then I remember and it's like being kicked in the stomach.

I curl away toward the wall, pulling my knees in until I'm as small as I can be, and I wrap the duvet around me and close my eyes.

I can't do this. I can't do any of it.

I need to see Leah and make sure she's okay, but she's in the hospital and I just can't face the lights, the sounds, or Mum. I also need to get to Mabel, make sure she's okay, and that I can do.

My jodhpurs are inside out on the floor. I turn them the right way around, pulling an old work fleece of Dad's out of the bottom drawer. I take my keys out of the back pocket of yesterday's jeans and my phone falls out.

I take the phone with one finger and thumb. I don't want to look at it. It slips and falls onto the carpet because my hands are shaking and I realize the battery is most likely dead, anyway. I don't want to turn it on and read the messages inside it. I don't need to see them to imagine what they say.

You selfish bitch, what were you thinking, bringing a horse to the beach.

You don't deserve a horse.

You should be reported for animal cruelty.

You don't deserve friends.

You're a bad person.

This is all your fault.

It's all your fault.

It's all my fault.

I put it in my pocket and creep downstairs. It's still early and there's no sound from Lisa. I write her a note to say I've gone to the stables and slide out of the front door so quietly that even Withnail doesn't notice.

It's harder to cycle than I expected. My muscles are aching from running along the shore road yesterday and I'm fighting to concentrate. Nothing's working properly. It's like I've got tunnel vision and as I cycle across the empty street a taxi blares its horn at me in the silence. I don't know where it came from, but it almost hit me. I keep going. I've got to get to the stables, got to make sure Mabel is safe.

As I turn toward the yard, I realize what I have to do.

I pull up at the corner and take the phone from my pocket, and I drop it between the metal slats of the drain cover and wait half a second. There's a plop and a splash as it falls down into the sewage system, and I know that I never need to look at it again.

"What the hell are you doing here?"

Polly is already in Mabel's stable, bent down on one knee, a white cotton wound dressing between her teeth. She wraps it around Mabel's foreleg and holds it in place while she tries to find the end of the bandage.

"Can I help?"

I feel as if I'm an intruder. Mabel turns to look at me for a moment, her eyes liquid brown and trusting, and I feel sick with guilt and shame.

"I've got it," says Polly, and she deftly wraps the bandage around and around. It stays in place by some kind of magic.

Polly straightens up and looks at me.

"Grace, the best help you could give right now is to get some bloody rest. Why aren't you in bed?"

"Couldn't sleep."

And she looks at me and shakes her head.

"I'm sorry." I whisper the words.

"Don't even go there," says Polly.

"But I am."

"I know," she says, and she smiles at me as if nothing has happened. "Where's your mum?"

She doesn't know. In Polly's world, all that we're dealing with is a horse that's been lucky to get away with superficial cuts and bruises, and an owner that doesn't deserve her.

"Hospital."

"What?" Polly's face registers shock and she bends down to pick up the vet kit. "Come on, you need to tell me what's happened. Is everyone okay?"

I nod.

We sit in the tack room and I spill out everything that's happened since I left. Polly makes coffee, with two huge spoonfuls of sugar and she hands it to me, shaking her head.

"You look a mess, Grace. Did you sleep last night?"

I did, but it was a weird, tangled swirl of nightmares and half rememberings. And now I'm phoneless, terrified about Leah, terrified about what's going on with the friends I had—and lost—and terrified about . . . well, everything. Life just feels as if it's too much to deal with.

"You need a break, Grace." I see her watching my hands, which are shaking. The trembling that started last night is back again. "Seriously, I can watch Mabes for you. Go and sleep or something."

"I can't sleep in the daytime."

Polly swigs the last of her coffee and puts the mug down with a thump on the metal draining board. She looks at me sideways, putting her hands on the small of her back and stretching. I think she's tired from looking after Mabel when she's already got loads of work to do, and I feel guilty about that too.

"Well, you don't need me to tell you that you're not safe around here when you're in this state. You're a liability, and we're already one horse down."

Her phone bleeps and she pulls it out and checks the screen.

"It's your mum. I'll tell her I'm giving you a lift back once I've done morning stables."

"But my bike—"

I start to protest but close my mouth when I see the expression on her face. It's not one I want to argue with.

Mabel's stiff this morning. I take her out of her box and lead her across to the tiny paddock where the Shetland ponies—restricted from eating too much grass so they don't get laminitis—are normally kept. We've led them into the outdoor arena where they're beetling about, hovering up the stray shoots of grass that have grown around the fence posts. I feel shame and guilt washing over me as each of Mabel's legs move clockwork slowly toward the field. My face flushes hot red and I feel prickly in my skin, like there's someone sitting just out of sight, watching me, judging me. Mabel moves as if all her joints are needing to be oiled. When I close the gate, she walks carefully toward the water trough, sniffing it gently. All her spark and fire are gone.

I did that to her. I turn away, her headcollar in my hand, and walk back toward the yard. Doubt creeps into my mind. I can't remember if I closed the gate properly—I turn back to check, and I've pulled the gate shut but forgotten to slide the bolt across. With trembling hands, I click it into place, the rusted metal stiff and unyielding.

Polly's right. I'm no use here either.

∘∘∘

"You gave me a shock," says Lisa. She pulls the door open before I've even made it up the steps into the front porch. "Thanks," she calls to Polly, giving her a wave. The little Corsa rolls off in a cloud of faulty exhaust smoke.

Inside the house, there's a smell of disinfectant and furniture polish. Lisa's left a bottle of it sitting on the dresser, and I catch sight of an upturned bucket on the draining board in the utility room sink. She's hoovered too, and the place looks spotless, the way it did when Grandma left. There's a thin shaft of sunlight coming in through the porch window and the tiny specks of dust she's scared up from the furniture are suspended there in midair, minuscule pieces of the world. I watch them and think about us suspended in the universe, hanging here, waiting to be blown around. Yesterday morning everything was one thing and now it's another and I don't like the way things keep changing. I don't want to be moved about.

Anna's mum breaks through the silence: "I've just spoken to your mum," and I realize I'm standing staring, my mouth hanging half-open, my arms dangling uselessly by my sides. It doesn't feel like home with everyone gone and everything changed. I wish hard that Dad might hear my thoughts and magic himself from the frozen wilderness to be back here. I want him to come and make us pancakes and have Radio Four droning on in the background and Mum yelling at him for leaving bloody coffee cups all over his desk in the study. I want Leah dancing about in tennis shoes and winding me up with Megan, not lying in a hospital bed wired up to machines because she's almost killed herself with alcohol poisoning. I want—

"You're away in a dream," Lisa continues. And she looks at me searchingly. "What are you thinking? Don't worry, sweetie, everything's going to be okay."

I look at her, and I know my face is set like a stone. I can't make it into the right shape to keep her happy. I don't even *know* what the right shape would be. I just want everything to go away.

She smiles at me again. I can't help feeling that she's not quite sure what to do with me, like she's worried I might burst into tears or flames or something. She's got a strange expression underneath the smiley crinkles in the corners of her eyes.

And then I realize I know what it is. She knows Anna hates me for what happened, and she doesn't know how to tell me. And she's having to be here to be polite and do the right thing because she's friends with Mum, and—my skin prickles again at the thought and I realize that I'm tapping thumb to finger to thumb again in a rhythm. I catch her watching my fingers moving, and I quiet them so they're still, but the movement just shifts and I *tap tap tap* inside.

When I was little and they sent me to the Jigsaw center, they used to try to get me to stop. *Quiet hands, Grace*, they'd say, and they'd hold them in my lap, smiling. And I'd want to scream at them that it's like having a motor ticking over inside me, and if I don't fidget something in my head wants to explode, but I couldn't find the words. And right now my head wants to explode. I get a sudden urge to pick up the bottle of furniture polish and throw it against the mirror and watch it smash into a thousand razor shards. I squeeze my hand into a ball so the fingernails dig into my palms.

I can't do that, anyway. Withnail would stand in the broken glass and I'm already the worst animal owner in the world. But that's what people seem to do. It happens on television all the time. They just pick things up and they throw them and they walk away and somehow it works out for them. And I still can't get the rules. I watch and I try to absorb it, and I try to get it right and hang out at the park and fit in, and somehow I break everything. Not glass, but people. And lives.

"Anyway, the doctor's happy with Leah's blood work. They're on the way back. Shouldn't be long." She picks up the duster that's lying on the dresser and folds it into a neat square, smoothing it out with her fingers before placing it down carefully on the shiny wood. "I'll put the kettle on, shall I?"

CHAPTER TWENTY-NINE

know I'm supposed to want to hug Leah when she walks back in with Mum. But she's pale and sick and they both smell alien, of hospitals and bleach and smooth metal bed frames and plastic pipes and fear. Leah's got bruised dark shadows under her eyes and her hair is dull and lifeless, tied back with an unfamiliar purple hair band. She looks at me and I can't tell what she's thinking. The expression on her face is strange and it scares me.

"Grace . . ." Mum begins, but I step backward and pick up Withnail as a shield, holding her in my arms. She squirms, but I don't let her go, rubbing under her ears until she stops protesting and starts purring, even though she doesn't want to.

"Morning," says Leah.

Lisa is standing in the hall and she's picked up the duster again and is twisting it in her hands, watching. I think she looks like she wants to leave. I think that I'd quite like to leave too. I wonder if I could just walk away from everyone and everything and start again as a new person.

It's as if we're hanging in the air now, like the dust motes. We're suspended here in this strange, static atmosphere for a moment that seems to last for ages, and then—

"I could kill for a coffee," says Mum. And Lisa steps forward and hugs her, and Leah looks at me over her shoulder and half shrugs and I smile at her and let Withnail drop to the ground. She lands on featherlight feet and dances away to the top of the stairs, where she sits licking her front paws and watching.

"Leah, in you come to the kitchen," says Lisa, and I step back out of the way and watch them all go through. And again I feel as if I'm not part of this picture and I don't know how I'm supposed to behave. So I sit down on the stairs and I try not to think. And thoughts sneak into my head. I see Mabel lying on the beach and I feel a raw ache of guilt and panic, and I make that thought go away by opening my eyes and focusing really hard on the pattern on the carpet until my eyes go funny.

And then I close them again and see everyone in the distance waving their arms and shouting as I'm running. I remember how I turned back just once, and their arms were flailing in the air and the shouts were whipped away from their mouths so all I could see was angry faces, Anna's angry face, and I knew then that I had to get away.

And I open my eyes again because I don't want to see that in my head either. And then I close them again and I see Leah, ghostly white, lying still on the carpet. And I don't know how to make any of it disappear, and it frightens me.

ooo

Eventually, Lisa leaves. She smiles at me sitting folded up on the stairs and tells me to get some rest and not to worry about anything, which I think means that it doesn't matter that I've lost my best friend and I have to go back to school tomorrow and there will be nobody there who'll speak to me. I nod at her but don't speak. I think I've run out of words.

"I'm putting you in a shower, honey," says Mum to Leah, and as she passes me on the stairs she drops a hand on my head for a moment and looks at me and her face looks—quizzical, I think. "You all right there, darling?"

And I give a tiny little upward nod because I can't make words come out. It's like they've gotten stuck.

I don't speak all afternoon, and nobody notices. Mum comes through and says that Polly has told her she's looking after Mabel and she's fine and I nod again.

And I want her to ask me what's wrong. And I half want her to hold me in a cuddle and squeeze me tightly and tell me she loves me and that everything's going to be okay, but she's busy looking after Leah and I think she hasn't really noticed that I'm not okay. Or maybe she doesn't really care. But she doesn't seem to realize that my words have gotten stuck like paper gets jammed in a printer and I can't make a noise. I've shut down.

I sit on the stairs for so long that my legs go numb and ache. And I need to go to the bathroom, but I let the pain of that sit inside me too until I'm so desperate that my bladder feels as if it might burst. But I feel like I deserve that—to be uncomfortable and sore feels right. I sort of want to stop being. I go to my room once I've been to the bathroom and I sit down on the floor with my back to the wall, crunched up really tiny in the corner. My hands are freezing.

Sometimes I hear Mum taking Leah upstairs and the sound of her throwing up in the toilet. And then flushing and muttered words and kind noises, and then silence again.

I don't know how long I sit in my corner.

"Grace, dinner," Mum shouts.

I'm not hungry, I think. I can't open my mouth to say it because it's as if my lips have been stapled shut. I tip forward onto my hands and knees, and straighten up to standing. All my bones and muscles feel hard and unyielding. This is how Mabel feels, stiff-legged in her paddock.

I get halfway down the stairs and sit down.

"Come on, darling." Mum comes into the hall. She sounds more like her usual self, by which I mean she's nagging. "What have you been up to all afternoon? I bet you've been glued to that phone. Honestly, I tell you, things are going to change around here."

I get up and walk into the kitchen.

Leah's quiet too, but she wants to know how Mabel is. And Mum tells her how she ran away and how amazing Polly is being and how brave Mabel was for the vet and that she's got stitches in her leg and I just sit there listening.

"My God," says Leah, looking at me as if she hadn't spent the night in hospital. "Are you okay?"

And Mum looks across at me as if she's waiting for me to finish the story. She puts down her glass and tucks a strand of hair behind her ear. I push my chair away from the table because I can't sit through any more of this.

So Mum continues.

"When Anna rang me to tell me what had happened, I jumped in the car—thank God Eve and I hadn't actually made it into the cinema or I'd have had no reception."

I sit back down on my chair heavily.

"Where's Eve now?" Leah flicks me a conspiratorial look, and it's the first spark of her old self I've seen. She's been quiet and withdrawn until now—not just because she feels like shit (I assume she's got the mother of all hangovers) but also because at some point, when Mum finishes being lovely about this, she's going to be grounded from here to kingdom come.

Mum gives us an odd look. "Oh, we had a bit of a—"

Leah leans forward slightly. "A—what?"

"It was nothing," says Mum. "Bit of a difference of opinion, that's all."

My jaw unclenches slightly and I move it from side to side. It starts to ache.

Mum picks up her glass and spins it between her fingers. Normally, she'd have red wine, but I notice that it's sparkling water. I guess after the whole hospital thing she doesn't want us getting any ideas. After listening to Leah throwing up all afternoon, I don't think she has anything to worry about.

"So what happened?" Leah shoves her food around her plate a bit. She hasn't eaten anything yet, I notice. Nor have I, because my mouth is still superglued shut. Mum's done her usual stress thing and catered for a family of ten. There are dishes of vegetables and rice lined up right down the middle of the table.

"Oh." Mum's mouth twists sideways. "When I got the call from Anna, Eve told me to leave it. Said you'd be fine and you were old enough to sort yourselves out."

"Huh." Leah looks at me.

I don't say anything.

Mum and Leah chat about Eve and they don't seem to notice I'm not talking. I get up and clear the table after a while, and as I'm heading out of the door Mum says—

"You look exhausted, sweetheart. I'll be up in a moment. Want me to run you a nice bath?"

I shake my head.

When she comes into my room, I'm sitting perched on the end of the bed. I feel as if I've got a sour-tasting wave of tears and shouting threatening to break at any moment, but it's like the switch has been turned off and I can't find it. I'm rubbing my finger along the lines that pattern the woolen throw that lies over the end of the bed.

"Grace," Mum begins. She puts an arm over my shoulders and it lies there, warm and heavy. "I want you to know that I'm not angry. Do you think I'm angry?"

I shake my head.

"Have you spoken to Anna?"

I shake my head again.

"She'll be worrying about you, I'm sure."

"I don't think so," I say, and my voice sounds creaky and rusty, like it's been left out in the rain.

"Oh, honey," Mum says. "Have you had a falling-out?"

I look down at the bedspread and run three fingers side by side along the indentations, watching them rise and fall as they follow the bulk of the crumpled duvet that lies underneath.

I don't say anything.

"We've all been a bit . . ." Mum bites at her thumbnail for a moment, looking at me thoughtfully. "It's been a bit all over the place this time, hasn't it?"

I look at her.

Yes.

"I've spoken to Grandma today about what's going on. And I think—she thought—we . . ." She pauses, as if she's nervous to say whatever it is, and she straightens out the pillowcase at the other end of my bed before she carries on talking, pulling out a crushed T-shirt that's been missing for ages from down the side of the bed.

"We thought as you've had a bit of a time of it, and Polly's happy to look after Mabel, maybe you could go down to Grandma's for a few days. Just get a change of scenery."

She doesn't know what to do with me. I'm not surprised, really, because I don't know what to do with me.

"I mean, of course, if you don't want to, that's okay, and I know you'll miss the first week back to school but we can tell them you're off sick and . . ." She's talking faster and faster, so I can't find a gap to respond.

"Fine," says my rusty voice.

ooo

Before I go, I sneak into Leah's room when she's in the shower. Mum's cleaned it up so it's all spotless and new bedcovers and even by Leah's (much tidier than mine) standards it looks perfect. I leave her my favorite bath bomb that I've been saving for a two-hour bath-and-book session, and the three pony books that Grandma gave me from Aunty Lou's room—the ones I guard with my life and won't normally let her touch. And I fasten my TARDIS key ring to her keys and write a note on a yellow sticky Post-it that says, "Try not to have any disasters while I'm gone," and a smiley face.

ooo

And that's how I end up alone on the train to Euston. I'm packaged up like a parcel, with a bag full of food and two new books I've wanted for ages (that's when I know Mum's feeling guilty, because normally I beg and beg for her to spend money on them and she tells me to go to the library and put a reservation in, complaining that my reading habit costs her a fortune and moaning on about how important it is to use your library). I'm at the window in a double seat with my bag next to me so nobody will sit there, and at the other end—"As soon as you open the door, darling, I'll be there"—Grandma will be waiting.

I could spend forever on trains. I watch the backs of houses in the rain, the gardens stuffed with trampolines and discarded ride-on cars, the neatly cut lawns and scruffy-looking yards full of scrap metal. We slow through towns where identical houses line up neatly back to back, reaching off in pairs into the distance. Through hills and trees and the flat nothingness of the middle of the country and then the never-ending squat gray warehouse buildings that seem to surround every city. I'm lulled to a half-sleeping state by the sound of the train on the tracks and the hum of people talking, but not to me.

I don't even read my books. I just stare and stare. When Mum discovered I'd lost my phone—I didn't tell her what had really happened, because I suspect that if she knew I'd deliberately drowned the expensive phone I'd begged for just a few months ago she'd have gone mad—she insisted on giving me the ancient Nokia brick we call the punishment phone. Normally, it's only handed out when our phones have been confiscated for bad behavior, and being forced back to an unresponsive gray-black screen is torture. Now, because I don't want to know what anyone is saying to me or about me, it's heaven. Because I know that what's happened will be everywhere and when school goes back tomorrow there'll be a sea of whispers, and eyes rolling over the crowds searching for me, waiting to land on my face so they can turn to one another.

Did you hear what Grace did? Can't believe she'd run off like that and leave her horse. Horse? I can't believe she left Gabe's cousin lying there. Gabe Kowalski? Can't believe she was hanging around with him, anyway.

∘∘∘

"It'll have all blown over by the time you get home," Grandma says sagely when she collects me at Euston. I follow her like an obedient puppy as we make our way through the people and the smells and the banging bells and noises and the clatter of announcements and down through the silver metal-smelling escalator and onto the tube to change stations.

I sleep through the next train journey that takes us down to the seaside, where Grandma's house sits, set back from the road, looking over the pebbles of the beach. It feels so far away from home. The sky is different here, the light brighter somehow. I stand at the window of the sitting room and look out to sea, imagining if I stare hard enough I might catch a glimpse of France in the distance. And I wonder if I could just wade into the sea and swim there, and start walking, and keep walking, and just disappear.

CHAPTER THIRTY

wake in Aunty Lou's bedroom and it smells of old books and dusty wallpaper. Grandma doesn't believe in duvets, and I'm compressed under a pile of thick linen sheets and heavy blankets and there's a smell of toast coming underneath the door and it feels safe, and familiar, and I half wonder if I could just stay here and go to school around the corner and just pretend my old life didn't exist.

I get up, pull on the bathrobe that's hanging on the back of the glass-paneled bedroom door, and make my way downstairs.

Grandma is reading the paper at the breakfast table. And she's got everything laid out, just like she always does. There's toast sitting neatly in a rack, and the marmalade is in a jar with a saucer and a little silver spoon beside it. The butter's not in the plastic tub with the foil crinkled back and crumbs all around the edges—it's a neat shape in a white china butter dish. And there's a crisp white tablecloth with flowers around the edges. Grandma embroidered them herself when she was first married.

"There's tea in the pot, dear," says Grandma, looking at me over the top of her glasses. "And I've made some fruit salad if you'd like that first before toast. It's through the hatch, there, look—"

She motions to the old-fashioned wooden hatch that opens up above the dining table and into the kitchen. Grandma's house is like stepping back in time. It's safe here. Newspaper crosswords and half days working in the charity shop and deadheading roses and none of that social-media nonsense, darling. I realize with a lurch that it's the first day back at school.

"You know . . ." Grandma folds the paper and watches me as I scoop up fruit salad and put it in my bowl. I'm starving suddenly, and I feel as if I could eat the whole lot. "Your dad and your aunty Lou got into some pretty disastrous scrapes when they were teenagers too."

"Not like this," I say, and I feel the corners of my mouth turning downward.

"Oh, just like this." Grandma nods her head. She takes off her reading glasses and slides them into a case as she continues. "And it was always the end of the world, especially for your aunty Lou. Nothing was ever just a bit of a problem. It was all or nothing with her."

I think of Aunty Lou and her amazing whitewashed house in Spain and her cats and her horses and her dream life.

"But she's so . . ." I scrabble for the word. Grown-up, I think, probably. Together. Cool. Calm. All the things I'm not and I will never be.

"She wasn't always. I tell you, we had some disasters in our day. When your granddad was alive, he had to drive to Carlisle to rescue her once. She fell out with a friend and sneaked on board the bus to Inverness."

The clock above the fireplace chimes the half hour. Grandma's dog, Elsa, looks up, still lying flat on the hearth rug. Anticipating her walk, she gives a hopeful beat of her tail. She's a creature of habit, just like Grandma. Just like me, I think.

"Anyway . . ." Grandma smiles again, and there's a far-off look on her face, as if she's remembering something. "I think what I'm trying to tell you, my dear, is that it's okay to get things wrong. We're all still learning."

"Not you," I say.

"Oh, even me," says Grandma. "The day you stop learning, my love, is the day you stop living."

I can't imagine Grandma, who seems to know everything about everything, and is a proper grown-up sort of grown-up, never being lost and confused and not knowing what to do.

"Look at your mum," she carries on. "Between you and me, I had no idea what to do about that Eve. I could see she was a bad influence—my goodness, I had enough trouble with your aunty Lou when she was growing up—but I couldn't work out how to tell your mum I didn't like her much."

"No." I swirl my teaspoon around in my cup. "She wasn't exactly . . . nice."

"She showed her true colors in the end, though," Grandma said. "Where was she when your mum needed her?"

I think back to Lisa turning up on the doorstep when Leah was being tended to by the paramedics. Mum had been out with Eve. She'd left her to come searching for me after Mabel ran off. I didn't even think about where Eve had gone.

"She wasn't interested in your mum the way she is now. She just wanted her the way she remembered her—carefree and wanting to have a good time. And I'm not surprised Julia enjoyed that. It's pretty hard work being a parent, and she's been doing it all by herself for far too long. Your father needs to realize that."

"He doesn't even know what's happened," I realize, thinking out loud.

"Oh, he does. Believe me, he does." Grandma shakes her head, and I think she looks disapproving.

ooo

We do Grandma things all day. I put on one of her big old dog-walking coats and we take Elsa along the beach. She canters along at the edges of the path, her legs loping along, covering the ground, a piece of driftwood in her mouth. She's gentle and beautiful, like a huge wild wolf dog, but I watch as other people skirt around her cautiously, fearful of her German shepherd reputation, though she couldn't be kinder.

We stop and have tea—always tea, so much tea—at the little cafe that's open all year round, and I crunch down along the pebbles of the beach in search of the perfect skimming stone, remembering holidays we've spent here when Dad's been around. When Elsa's tired out, we take her back home and Grandma settles down in front of the television to watch her favorite program. I have a bath and stay in it for hours, reading my book. I don't get out until my fingers and toes are pruned in the water and the edges of the pages are all speckled with damp.

We eat cottage pie for dinner and sit in the evening watching *Coronation Street* and eating chocolates from a tin Grandma's probably had sitting there for months. Elsa balances her head on my lap as I read the last of my book and I look up from the story world as it ends, surprised to discover that I'm here in Kent and not back home in my bedroom. I'd forgotten for a time, and the memory of why I'm here settles like a stone in my stomach again. I kiss Grandma good night and take myself upstairs to bed.

Another two days pass. I don't even know what I've done with the ancient brick phone. There's nobody to call me, and life back home feels like a vague memory. I miss Mabel all the time, though, with an ache that twists inside me. But I shut it off, telling myself that she loves Polly too, and that she's being cared for and looked after and that I'm better off here, away from everything else. And I miss Leah too, of course, and Anna (will she ever forgive me?), and Gabe (God, I don't even want to know what he thinks of me now). I don't want to go home.

Mum calls and I hear Grandma talking to her about routines and tennis training. In the silences between the words I can hear her asking, but not asking, if Eve has been around. Telling Mum how amazing she thinks she is and what a good job she does. Telling her Dad will be back soon and that she needs to book a spa break or something lovely. And then she hands the phone to me.

"Leah," she says.

"Hey," I say. We don't really do phone conversations, so this is a new one.

"Hello," says Leah. "What's happening in Grandma World?"

And I breathe a sigh of relief because she sounds normal and Leahish and not the wispy echo of herself that she was when I left.

"Nothing much," I say. "What's happening in Grounded for All Eternity World?"

Leah snorts with laughter. "Ah yes, that."

"I assume you are, right?"

"Yeah, well, I haven't exactly asked if I can go out."

"So what've you been doing?" I picture Leah scrubbing the floors on her hands and knees, but decide that she's probably gotten off relatively lightly. "Seriously, Lee, you gave us a massive fright."

"I gave *me* a massive fright."

"So you're not planning on going out with Lily Carmichael and her gang in the near future?"

"Uh . . ." There's a pause, and I imagine Leah shaking her head violently. "No. Not so much. No. I don't think we're destined to be best friends."

I don't say it, but I'm relieved.

"So how did you . . ."

"End up unconscious with cider poisoning?" Leah finishes my sentence. "I dunno. Mum wasn't in, Lily got a load of it from somewhere, we were drinking in the sitting room when Mum was out with Eve, and . . ."

She sort of trails off. I think again about Lily and the rest of them walking off and leaving Leah at the house, so drunk she couldn't even walk or think, and I want to kill them for putting her in danger.

"They're not your friends." I think of Anna and her kind face and I feel a wave of sadness that I've messed things up too.

"Er, no," says Leah. "Don't worry, I've had Anna and all that lot doing the surrogate-big-sister bit on them."

"Anna?"

"Yeah, she sorted it with—oh, hang on, Meg's here. Got to go. We're having a Harry Potter marathon with popcorn and pizza. See you."

And she's gone before I can even say good-bye, so some things really have gone back to normal.

○○○

I wake up on the fourth morning when the sun shines in on my face through a gap in the curtains. It feels late, later than usual.

"Morning, sleepyhead," says Grandma. She's outside the kitchen door in the garage that joins on the side, folding washing as she pulls it out of the machine. She puts the last pillowcase on the top of the pile and picks up a clothes pin bag from the hook on the wall.

"Would you like to help me hang these out, as we've got a bit of sun?"

Only Grandma would fold up washing before she hangs it out. I pick up the basket for her and carry it out to the patio. The last of the climbing roses are spilling petals onto the lavender bushes below them. The colored flagstones remind me of games of hopscotch when Leah and I were little. I hand the washing to Grandma, one item at a time. There are birds singing in the big fuchsia bush where we used to collect the flowers, which looked like little ballerinas. It's so peaceful here, and I want to stay forever.

There's the ringing of a bell and clamoring as we turn to go inside. The wind carries the sound of the secondary school across the playing field that backs the garden, and my knees go liquidy with fear for a moment. I don't want to go back, but I can't not. And that's a terrifying feeling.

I pick up the empty washing basket and follow Grandma back into the house.

"The mail gets later every day," Grandma says from the hall. I climb in over the step and into the kitchen. My stomach is growling for breakfast and I'm dying for some coffee.

"One for you," says Grandma, putting a huge, fat, pale blue envelope on the table where I'm about to sit down.

"Me?"

I look at the writing on the front and recognize it instantly. It's Anna's mad scribble, and there's a doodle of a horse on one corner, and a little bunch of flowers on the other. The back is covered in rude Shakespeare quotes, and my heart gives a little skip.

Grandma passes me a silver sword thing.

"It's a letter opener, darling," she says, when I look at her sideways as if she's gone bonkers. I slide it into the top corner and it tears through the paper.

A picture slips out onto the table. Anna has cut out a photo of Taylor Swift and one of her girlfriends holding hands from *Heat* magazine or something, and stuck our heads over the top from the day we were sent to get passport photos and spent the fiver messing around in the booth instead. Her mum went mad at us and marched Anna back to the photographer's studio in town, where she chose the most hideous picture for her passport as revenge.

"You girls," says Grandma, laughing. "I'll just pop upstairs."

She leaves me at the table then and disappears out of the room, leaving me sitting on the edge of the armchair looking at the envelope. My heart is racing now. If Anna's sent this, she can't—

I pull out the gigantic card that's inside. There's a picture of a guinea pig wearing a pair of goggles on the front.

Dear Gracie of Moo, Anna begins, in her mad, spidery, totally untidy handwriting.

*I am slightly unimpressed that you have gone AWOL, leaving me to deal
with the twin horrors of (a) Holly Carmichael, who is almost PURPLE with horror
and envy that An Exciting Thing happened in the holidays with Leah and she isn't
the center of attention because her sister was caught up in it and (b) Miss Martin,
who has redirected her hatred of you in my direction as you missed double math
on Monday morning.*

I pull a face at this. But my heart is galloping with excitement and
I feel the most Grace-ish I've felt in what feels like forever.

*Mum and your mum are worried that you've gone into a terminal decline
like Ophelia in* Hamlet *and you're currently making plans to sail off to your doom
festooned in flowers (was that the Lady of Shalott? I get confused), but I am assuming (never assume, Dad says helpfully, it makes an Ass of U and Me—which
is officially the most hideous bit of Dad-speak in the history of the planet and I
apologize profusely) that you are just hibernating and getting better and recover-
ing and stuff. Although it might be nice if you answered your messages. But you've
been offline since forever, so I am assuming (never assume, etc.) that you are in
an internet-free zone or even banned forever. Hence getting your grandma's ad-
dress in a fit of Astonishing Genius and writing you an actual letter like a Victorian
chum.*

*I have many things to tell you, but I daren't put them on here in case it's in-
tercepted (but please note that one of those things is very much skateboard-
related). Please send back an owl or telegram or whatever it is the young people
are doing these days.*

I put the card down for a moment and plop from the arm of the
chair down onto the cushions.

The trouble with people is they don't tell you how they feel in words
of one syllable or less, so you always imagine the worst. The trouble
with being me is I don't know how to ask because my words get stuck.

For the last few days, I've been living in a world where I don't have
an Anna anymore, and I'm just on my own. And now I'm in a world

where there's definitely an Anna, and she's definitely not angry with me, and because she's so nice and easygoing and all the things I like her for, she doesn't even seem to be angry. I don't understand.

I pick up the card again and realize there's a long PS scribbled on the back.

Also. I know what you're like because you're my favorite GMoo. Also I bumped into Leah in the science corridor (OMG seriously, I can't believe the whole Cidergate thing . . .) on Monday and she told me your mum was worried you were making secret plans to emigrate or move to your Grandma's house. Nobody is angry with you. In the interest of disclosure, you were the major topic of conversation from first thing on Monday until first break . . .

I feel a wash of horror turning my skin icy cold, then hot, in a split second.

Well, partly you for running off like that, but mainly Holly Carmichael (and her being a complete cream-faced loon who could have caused massive kite-based tragedy and killed Mabel AND Gabe's cousin Marek just because she can't cope with the attention not being on her),

I look away from the card for a moment, letting the words sink in.

but then Alison Fairgrave turned up late with her hair dyed mermaid blue and her eyebrow pierced and she was supposed to be sent home but her mum started arguing with the head of tenth grade in the playground and—well, I'll tell you the rest later. Oh, and if you want the news on everything else—you'll have to turn your bloody phone on. XOXOXOXOXO (etc.) me x

p.p.s. (!!!) Gabe says hi.

I don't know what to do with any of myself. Inside of me I'm skipping about and doing a celebration dance and I'm crying because I'm so relieved that not everything is awful and I still have a best friend after all and maybe, just maybe, I have a boy who might like me, a little bit, who I like, a little bit. Or even a bit more than that. And another part of me is angry because life is so complicated and nobody tells you anything and there's so much of being human that's about unspoken stuff and presuming and *well, I just thought you knew* and I never know anything until it's too late and I've swum to France and given up my old life and started a new one. Or tried to persuade Grandma to enroll me in the secondary school across the field, which I actually hinted at yesterday.

I smooth the card out on the table and read it all over again. Then I go upstairs and find the ancient brick phone and switch it on.

Grandma seems delighted that I have a card from Anna. She leaves me watching television and disappears off to the shops to buy the ingredients to make her famous pineapple cheesecake for pudding, which is Dad's favorite, and then later, when the kitchen windows are steamed up with baking and dinner and the house smells so delicious I think my stomach might digest itself (but she won't let me have anything to eat, because she's old-fashioned and says it'll spoil my dinner, which it absolutely will not), she picks up the car keys again.

"Forgot pineapple," she says, and is gone in a second before I have a chance to say that, no, I saw four tins in the pantry.

I'm sneaking a handful of chocolate chips from the plastic tub on her baking shelf when there's a bang as the front door shuts and a thud, as if someone's dropped something heavy on the carpet.

"You okay?" I shout as I open the door to the hall.

"Fine, thank you," says my dad, with the biggest, beardiest, scruffiest grin you could possibly imagine.

"*Dad!*" I squeal, and jump up and down on the spot like I'm five.

He catches me midjump and squishes me into the tightest squeeze. He smells of outside and cold things and Dad-ness and home and being safe.

"Why are you here?"

"Because I just got off a flight in Gatwick, and got on the train down here to see my favorite big girl instead of heading up to the studios to pick up my car," he says, still smiling.

"Come out of the hall, you two," Grandma says, shooing us through into the little sitting room.

And we eat dinner until we can't move and Dad tells Grandma that after months of eating whatever he could get his hands on this is the best meal he's ever tasted, and Grandma says that he should probably save that line for when he gets home to his wife, because she needs all the moral support she can get after the time she's had.

And Dad frowns a bit and looks at me.

"Have you three been having a bit of a bad time?"

And I look at Grandma because I'm not sure what I'm supposed to say to that, and she sort of gives me a little nod, and I say—

"I don't like it when you go away."

And he nods then.

And Grandma says—

"I think the balance is a bit off, Graham . . ."

And Dad nods again and shifts in his chair and I think he's feeling a bit uncomfortable and that he preferred it when we were all eating cheesecake and smiling and talking about the polar bears he'd seen.

"Anyway," says Grandma, "that's for another day. Let's get the jet lag over with first, hmm?"

CHAPTER THIRTY-ONE

"It's a shame they don't hand out rule books when you have children," says Dad, out of the blue.

We're on a motorway somewhere on the way home, and I'm eating all the black wine gummies from the packet I've found in his glove compartment. The back of the car is full of Dad's equipment, and my bag's squashed on the top, so you can't see out of the back window.

"It's a shame they don't hand out rule books when you're born," I point out through a mouthful of wine gums.

"Yeah, well." Dad runs a hand through what's left of his hair. It stands up in little spiky tufts. It's definitely getting thinner. He'd say that was the stress of having me and Leah, but if that were the case Mum ought to be as bald as a coot.

(Are coots even bald? I must look that up.)

"Thing is, Grace, your mum's been so determined to do the right thing by you and Leah, and I haven't exactly been around much."

"You're working," I protest, thinking of the three of us sitting down together to watch his programs with the fire lit and popcorn and Withnail curled up between us.

"Yeah, but Mum needs to get out and have a life of her own, too. And I've been so wrapped up in my career—"

He chews on his thumbnail, holding on to the steering wheel with one hand.

I realize he's not saying anything that Eve didn't say. I turn so my forehead is resting on the cold of the glass and watch the cat's eyes whizzing past in a blur. It's not Eve I hated—it's the change. I don't want Mum stuck at home bored to death, and we can manage perfectly well—Anna's mum works, after all. I feel my old friend guilt settling down on my lap. Hello, here we are again.

"She said she wasn't going to go for the interview after—after what happened with Leah."

We'd been driving to the station when she told me. She'd been insistent that the idea had left town along with Eve, and that she wasn't making any plans. I couldn't help thinking she had a look on her face that didn't match the words she was saying, but I didn't know what to say about that, so I just kept quiet.

"Yeah, and I've told her she needs to think about what she wants. The whole family has revolved around me for long enough."

I look at Dad, who is rubbing at his beard.

"You're going to stay home and Mum's going to work?"

"Uhh"—he pulls a face—"not quite. But I've taken far too much for granted, and I hadn't realized—not until last night when I was talking to your Grandma—just how close I came to losing everything."

"You?" I say, realizing they must have stayed up talking long after I disappeared upstairs to text Anna on the ancient phone of doom.

"Yep." His voice sounds a bit flat. "Look, darling—we didn't want to make a big thing of it, but when I went away last time Mum and I had been talking about splitting up."

And it all falls into place. I think of the half-finished comments Mum kept making, and the remarks about needing to stand on her own two feet, and I feel a bit silly that I didn't work it out for myself.

And then I wonder where *she* fits into everything.

"And what about Eve?"

"Oh, I think she'd be quite happy if your mum didn't have the three of us hanging around."

"You mean she . . ." I turn around in my seat to look at him, wondering if I've gotten their friendship all wrong. Does Eve have a *crush* on Mum?

Dad shakes his head. "No, nothing like that." He laughs a bit. "But I know Eve of old. She likes getting her own way, and even more than that, she's the queen of divide and conquer."

And it makes sense. She's like Holly Carmichael, who seems to take pleasure in watching things break apart. Eve didn't want us in the way of her friendship with Mum, which is why when it all hit the fan and everything went wrong she basically asked Mum to choose between us and her. And Mum chose us.

CHAPTER THIRTY-TWO

We drive through town. I am trying to remind myself of calm blue things and *ommm* and inner peace and all is well. But even with evil Eve vanquished and Dad coming back to cheer Mum on to get a job and Leah doing tennis and netball and general sportsing nightly (and put off alcohol, from what Dad says, for the rest of her life) I feel sick. Sick, sick, sick.

I've got to go to school on Monday and deal with everything. People are going to look at me with their eyes burning holes in me and I haven't even let myself think about the other thing. The thing I'm not mentioning. Well, the boy.

"I figured you'd probably want to check on Mabel, so we'll just nip into the stables first," says Dad, flicking the indicator to turn right toward the yard.

I feel a flirrup of nerves in my stomach. I'm worried Mabel might have forgotten me and I'm worried Polly is going to have stopped being nice and decided I'm a neglectful sort of owner who swans off on holiday, except I can hear a voice in my head (it's a sensible sort of voice, and I don't know where it's come from, but I like it) reminding me that, no, Grace, you had a major meltdown and you needed a break, and that's okay. And I take a breath and sit up a bit straighter and I feel as if actually being down at Grandma's has changed me a little bit. That maybe I've realized that it's not just me that messes up, that nobody really knows what they're doing. And I feel quite impressed with myself for that.

It won't last, I'm sure, but it'll do for now.

And then we pull into the yard and there's something taped to the wooden door frame above Mabel's box. And I get out of the car and step toward it and I pull my glasses off for a moment and rub them on my T-shirt because I'm not sure I can see right.

But when I put them back on, it's there.

WELCOME BACK, GRACE, it says on a banner covered in stars.

And there's a skittering of hooves and a snort and Mabel's head appears over the stable door and she whinnies at me with her eyes bright and her ears pricked with excitement and she nods her head up and down and I realize that she's got something plaited in her mane and I get closer and I see it's blue hair extensions from Claire's Accessories and I burst out laughing, and—

"Oh God, you're not meant to be here yet—I haven't painted her feet," says Anna, who pops out from the tack room with a pot of blue face paint and a brush.

"Just as bloody well," says Polly gruffly, but she's laughing, and she puts a hand on my shoulder and I turn around to look at her. "Thank God you're back. Your friends have been *helping*, and quite frankly I think they might be insane."

"Friends?" I say, looking at her and frowning.

And Gabe's head pops up from behind the stable door and his face looks pink and he's actually *blushing*.

"Well, he can stay," says Polly. "Turns out he can muck out and everything." She grins at Gabe, who unfastens the stable door and slips out. Mabel leans her head across his shoulder, whiffling for treats the way she does with me.

"Hi," says Gabe, and he smiles, and I smile right back at him.

"We missed you," says Anna.

And nobody rushes forward and hugs me, and I am glad about that, because it's more than enough to take in all the stuff that's happening and all the stuff that's happened.

"She's healing really well," says Polly. "Come and have a look."

I step forward toward Mabel's box, and Anna does a little skip of excitement and puts the face paint down ("I should think so too," mutters Polly darkly) and follows us. Gabe steps back out of the way, but I pass him close enough to notice he gives me a look that is so kind and lovely it makes my breath catch in my throat. He's got a piece of wood shaving stuck in his hair, and when I walk into Mabel's box I realize he's made it look perfect.

Mabel steps back politely and allows Polly to push her gently on the shoulder so she turns to face the light. I can see that even in a few days the scratches and cuts have healed. The bandage is gone from her foreleg, and her coat is shining. She looks like my horse again.

"I'm sorry," I whisper to Mabel, lifting her long mane so my breath catches in the soft hairs of her ears.

"You don't need to say it," says Polly. Gabe and Anna are standing with Dad by the stable door looking out into the yard, laughing and chatting as if they were all the best of friends. They're waving to someone.

I don't know what to do with all this.

And Polly continues, "We're human, Grace. Screwing stuff up is what we do best."

And Dad, who I thought wasn't listening, turns around to look in at us.

"It's the only way we learn."

There's a thump as Leah leaps on him from behind, and Mum joins her a moment later, and I watch the three of them hugging, but I don't feel like I'm left out this time. I feel okay.

ooo

I feel *so* okay that I suggest that we all go out for dinner that evening, me and Anna and Gabe and Leah and Dad and Mum. All of us.

And Dad makes embarrassing dad jokes, and the waiter offers us the wine menu and Mum suggests he give it to Leah as she's the expert. And Anna and Gabe laugh and point out Archie, who flies past the pizza place on the way to the floodlit skate park. Gabe keeps looking at me and blushing slightly when I meet his eyes. And I keep blushing when I catch *his* eye. And Mum and Dad keep looking at us and grinning.

And when we go up to the salad bar, somehow I end up standing there beside Gabe and he looks at me and says, "You okay?" and I say, "Yes." And I realize that I really am.

We go back to the table with our little bowls of salad and I notice Mum and Dad are holding hands and he keeps smiling at her. When she goes to the bathroom, he pulls her back for a moment so she lands on his lap and she laughs out loud and kisses him right there at the table, which ought to be embarrassing but actually, weirdly, isn't.

And the funny thing I've figured out is that sometimes when it seems like everything is falling apart, it's not the end—it's the beginning.

ACKNOWLEDGMENTS

This book was very quick to write, because it was a long time in coming. When my daughter Verity was very young, I realized very quickly that she didn't see the world the way other children did. It took a long, long time to get anyone to listen to me. Eventually, when she was thirteen, she got an autism diagnosis. And—surprised and not surprised at the same time, because the way she saw the world made perfect sense to me—the same year, I got an autism diagnosis too.

A year or so later, Grace popped into my head one day and started talking. And talking. I scribbled down her words, and realized she wasn't going to stop until I told her story—so here it is.

It's a testament to how much of a team effort a book really is that my acknowledgments page is miles long . . .

Thanks first of all to my dear friend Jax Blunt, who has cheered me along the way from the very first words to the final "Is this okay?" email. I couldn't have written Grace without you.

To Elise, for roller skates and introducing me to Judy Blume and adventures in the woods and a lifetime of friendship.

To Mum, Chris, and Zoe—thank you for being there, always. And to Mae—thank you for being one of my first readers.

To Ross—thank you for the tea, darling (sorry I forgot to drink it), and for everything you do. Verity, Archie, Jude, and Rory—I love you all so, so much and I am enormously proud of the strong, clever, kind people that you are. Thank you for making me laugh.

To early readers Tamsyn Murray, Ella Risbridger, Lucy Powrie, Amanda Colston, and Perdita Cargill, all of whom—at various stages of writing—gave me the courage to keep going.

Thanks to Rhiannon Adams for being there, night and day (usually night). And to Alice Broadway, Keris Stainton, and Hayley Webster for making everything better. To Cathy Bramley, Miranda Dickinson, and Kat Black—thank you for excellent hooting. And thanks to my lovely Caroline Smailes for being herself. I'm lucky to have you all.

Macmillan Children's Books—you lovely lot. It's so exciting to be part of the team seeing this book into the world. Thanks to my editor Rachel Petty for her amazing ability to see what a book needs to really shine. And huge thanks to Catherine, Kat, and George—you are all brilliant stars.

To the UKYA community, and the book bloggers who work so hard and make such a difference—your excitement and enthusiasm make this job so much fun. Thank you.

To everyone on Facebook, Instagram, and Twitter—thanks for giving me a reason to procrastinate, and for cheering me on. It's so lovely to share the process of every book with you all. Thanks especially to the #actuallyautistic tribe for making life better.

Amanda Preston, my agent, has been totally Team Grace from the moment I shared that very first snippet of her voice. Thank you— I'm so lucky to have you in my corner.

I'd also like to thank the staff of Bo'ness Library from years ago. They had no idea that the girl who visited every week and knew the teenage section by heart would one day become a writer. Libraries are magical places and we should treasure them.

Writing acknowledgments is the tricky bit—much harder than the book. Hopefully I haven't missed anyone out but, if I have, know that I am enormously grateful for you, and all the people who surround me who make life such an interesting adventure.

THANK YOU FOR READING THIS
FEIWEL AND FRIENDS BOOK.

THE FRIENDS WHO MADE

POSSIBLE ARE:

Jean Feiwel, Publisher

Liz Szabla, Associate Publisher

Rich Deas, Senior Creative Director

Holly West, Editor

Anna Roberto, Editor

Christine Barcellona, Editor

Kat Brzozowski, Editor

Alexei Esikoff, Senior Managing Editor

Kim Waymer, Senior Production Manager

Anna Poon, Assistant Editor

Emily Settle, Assistant Editor

Rebecca Syracuse, Associate Designer

Mandy Veloso, Production Editor

Follow us on Facebook or visit us online at mackids.com
OUR BOOKS ARE FRIENDS FOR LIFE.